Goodbye Summer

It is a summer quite unlike any other that Sasha has known. School is almost behind her, and ahead lies a threatening vista of ordinariness which makes her snatch at any chance of being different.

Sasha's parents seem to belong to a different world. She is sure they will never understand Nick, with his leather jacket and oily hands and utterly unreliable ways. But one thing is for sure – in the summer which says goodbye to childhood, Sasha is beginning to understand herself.

Goodbye, Summer

Falling leaf and fading tree,
Lines of white in a sullen sea,
Shadows rising on you and me,
Shadows rising on you and me.
The swallows are making them ready to fly,
Wheeling out on a windy sky,
Goodbye, Summer! Goodbye, goodbye,
Goodbye, Summer! Goodbye, goodbye.

Hush! A voice from the far away;
'Listen and learn,' it seems to say,
'All our tomorrows shall be as today,
All our tomorrows shall be as today.'
The cord is frayed, the cruse is dry,
The link must break and the lamp must die.
Goodbye to hope! Goodbye, goodbye!
Goodbye to hope! Goodbye, goodbye!

What are we waiting for? Oh, my heart,
Kiss me straight on the brows, and part!
Again, again! My heart, my heart!
What are we waiting for, you and I?
A pleading look, a stifled cry...
Goodbye for ever!
Goodbye for ever!
Goodbye, goodbye,
Goodbye.

F. PAOLO TOSTI

Goodbye Summer

ALISON PRINCE

A Magnet Book

Also by Alison Prince
in Magnet Books
Haunted Children
The Ghost Within

First published 1983 by Methuen Children's Books Ltd
Magnet paperback edition first published 1985
by Methuen Children's Books Ltd
11 New Fetter Lane, London EC4P 4EE
Reprinted 1987
Copyright © 1983 Alison Prince
Printed in Great Britain
by Richard Clay Ltd, Bungay, Suffolk

ISBN 0 416 51510 X

Acknowledgement is made to G. Ricordi and Co. (London) Ltd for
permission to reprint the Victorian song, 'Goodbye, Summer' by
F. Paolo Tosti on page 2. Copyright 1903 by G. Ricordi & Co.

Chapter 1

Liz and I were talking about men. It was a Sunday morning and I had just dyed my hair pink and tied it all up in rags like the photograph in *Cosmo*. We had the curtains drawn in my bedroom and the table-lamp shone dull red because I'd draped a silk shawl over it, and there were a couple of joss sticks burning in a little brass pot on the mantelpiece. We were very decadent that summer.

Liz was painting her finger nails gold. She wanted to turn on Radio One but I wouldn't let her. 'It's got no atmosphere,' I said, and she laughed. She knew what I meant; there was never any need to explain things to Liz.

She was such a funny-looking girl. We were both seventeen that summer but she might have been anything up to about thirty. She had pale gingery hair and pale eyelashes and a long face that was a bit hollow under the cheekbones – you could imagine her with a scarf tied round her head like the munition factory workers in those old war-time films. Her mouth was almost always open a bit and her teeth crossed in front. That Sunday morning she was wearing a black velvet smoking-jacket she'd bought in the Oxfam shop. It must have been made for some huge bloke because the sleeves hung down over her hands and it was vast, with curly patterns of black braid all down the front. Liz wore a pair of tattered old jeans under it, and a ribbed suntop that stayed up of its own accord, more or less. And a bow tie, daft idiot, tied round her neck like a Bunny girl. I was in my kimono that I'd bought at a jumble sale. It was almost dropping to pieces because it was so old, but it had embroidered dragons and chrysanthemums all over it, and great square sleeves, and it did up with a wide green sash that made my waist look tiny if I pulled it tight, and I loved it.

5

There was a bit in the *Sunday Times* about some thriller writer who said it was essential to his literary output to make love to a woman twice a day. It didn't matter who she was. Anyone would do. I thought it was awful.

Liz said, 'Perhaps it's like wanting to go to the loo. You know how you can't concentrate on anything until you've been.' And she looked at my hair in its rags and added, 'You look like a floor mop.'

I said, 'Fancy being some bloke's loo! I don't know how anyone could.' The idea absolutely turned me over, it seemed so disgusting, and I couldn't see how Liz could be so calm about it. She was only four months older than me but she seemed to know so much more. It was as if she'd grown up belonging to a club that I could never join; she belonged to what I thought of as the tough, mysterious people who talked about shift work and rent collectors and the Council coming to do the roof, and who went in the betting shops that had dark green paint on the windows so you couldn't see in. Liz understood all that and she somehow made me feel inferior although I was in a higher stream than her all the way through school. She had left as soon as she was sixteen and got herself a job as a trainee cook, and I was still stuck in the sixth form. I wanted to go to art school because I was mad about fashion and wanted to be a designer but the careers people said it was all different these days and you had to have qualifications for art same as anything else, so I had to stay on.

We were still arguing about the sexual habits of men when Mum shouted up the stairs to say she'd made some coffee. I shouted back to say thanks but before I could go down for it she was opening the door.

'It smells disgusting in here,' she said. 'Why have you got the curtains shut?'

'Because it's decadent,' I said. 'Dark and mysterious and private.' Somehow I could never help saying the things I knew would annoy her most.

She gave me a look and said, 'What have you done to your hair?' Then she swept the curtains back and the sunlight came bursting in. 'Oh, *Susan!*' she said. Anyone would think

6

I'd shaved it all off. She was lucky I hadn't – lots of girls were wearing bald heads that summer. And I did wish she'd stop calling me Susan. I'd been Sasha for over a year.

'It's only an experiment,' I told her. 'Look, it's the summer holidays, for goodness' sake. Nearly six weeks before I go back to the Upper Sixth fun factory. Didn't you ever do anything mad when you were young?'

She tucked a strand of her long, mousy hair back into its Alice band. Her mouth was tight at the corners. 'Of course I did,' she said. 'But at least we always looked nice.'

'*Nice!*' The word set me off on one of my harangues. I waved my arm at the view from the window which I'd been so carefully excluding. 'Like the *nice* garden and the *nice* fence and the *nice* neighbours. It makes me sick, all of it. That's why I keep the curtains shut – when I'm allowed to, that is!'

I thought she was going to lose her temper, but she didn't. 'All I can say to you, Susan, is that you'll get used to it,' she said. 'The same as I did. It's no good you thinking life is going to be beautiful and romantic, because it isn't.' She buttoned her mouth even tighter for a minute, and I hoped she was going out, then she added bitterly, 'If it wasn't beautiful for me, why should it be for you, I'd like to know? And bring your coffee cups down when you've finished.' She grabbed up all the various bits of the *Sunday Times* and marched out, but even then she turned back. 'And think who pays the electricity bill,' she snapped, and switched the table-lamp off. And banged the door behind her.

I switched the lamp on again and snatched the curtains shut. 'Oh, *God*,' I said, flinging myself down on the bed, 'I must get out of this place.'

'My mum's just as bad,' said Liz, wiggling her fingers in the air to dry her nails. 'I know she's had a hard time bringing me up on her own and all that, but she's got no idea how to enjoy herself. Can't relax.'

'It's all such a sell-out,' I said. I sat up and reached for my coffee. Now that my temper had blown itself out I felt depressed. It was always like that.

'Who sold out what?' enquired Liz.

'My mother. Your mother, too, probably. Thousands of women. They start like us – or I suppose they do – feeling they can do anything they want if they just put their mind to it. And then they meet some bloke and sell out all they've got for the sake of being given their measly housekeeping money each week. Honestly, I think women want their minds read.'

'Mine didn't do that,' said Liz rather smugly.

'No, but she was left holding the baby, wasn't she?' I said. I glared at her. Without meaning to, Liz always implied that having a tough upbringing made her a superior person. She needn't think she had a monopoly on hard times. 'At least your mum didn't get married,' I went on. 'Look at my parents. Dad off down the pub or got his nose in a book all the time, and Mum too touchy to talk to – they're just polite to each other, that's all, for the sake of convention. Call that a marriage? Call it a life?'

Liz didn't take much notice. She screwed the cap back on her bottle of nail varnish and sipped her coffee. Then she said, 'Tell you what. If you get yourself a job like you said you were going to, why don't we go away somewhere at the end of August? On our own. I've got a couple of weeks due.'

'I'm supposed to be going to blooming Aldeburgh,' I said gloomily. 'In September with the parents. There's absolutely nothing to do there. The only good thing is, it overlaps the beginning of term by four days. Dad had to have his holiday then to fit in with the other people at the Bank. You'd think now he's a manager he could have first pick, wouldn't you?'

Liz chuckled. 'I expect he said, "No, no, old chap, never mind about me",' she said. 'You know what he's like, all quiet and self-effacing. I like your dad, actually. I think he's sweet.'

'Yes, he is,' I said. 'But he's sweet in a funny sort of way. He doesn't really like people much – not people in general. Perhaps it's because he has to deal with them all day and he's sick of them. If anyone comes to the house he tries to sneak away so they won't know he's in, but if they actually hunt him down he's always terribly nice to them. I think he feels guilty about secretly not liking them.'

'Perhaps he just doesn't need anyone,' said Liz. She

grinned and added, 'Not like the thriller writer and his twice-a-day dose.'

That set me off again. 'If sex isn't special,' I said, 'then what is? It's a big thing to decide to do. It's like telling someone your innermost thoughts and dreams, letting them in to your innermost body.'

'It ought to be special,' Liz agreed, 'but I don't know that it is. I mean, if you don't mind people kissing you, why mind the rest? Nothing is a more personal part of you than your mouth.'

I looked at Liz's mouth with the teeth that crossed a bit in front, and remembered seeing her and Billy Ashburn kissing in the car park after that disco I went to with Roy Blakely. I hadn't liked Roy. There was something awful about his red wrists with pale hairs on them, and I had hoped to go home with Liz so as to get away from him. But she went on and on kissing Billy Ashburn with her head back and her eyes shut, so I had to go in Roy's car with him putting his hand on my knee all the way home. He had kissed me so long when we arrived that I felt as if I couldn't get my breath but I pretended to like it because I didn't want him to think I was just a kid. I'd been out with a good few boys since then, but always with a feeling that I rather hated it even if I was enjoying myself. But I'd never have admitted even to Liz that I felt like that. I was trying so hard to be grown up.

'I reckon it's like booze,' said Liz. 'The first drink is great and after that it's just the same again.'

'I drank an awful lot of sherry last Christmas,' I said. 'Mum was furious.' I was beginning to feel fraught. How were you supposed to know what to do? People droned on about what they did when they were young, but nobody had lived *my* life before. 'Anyway,' I said, 'I don't want anything to be the same again, over and over. How can you collect experience if you never do anything new?'

'Dead right,' said Liz. It was one of our great things, experience. We talked about it a lot. We collected it the way other people collected stamps. Liz picked up my brown mascara and unscrewed the top. 'Can I borrow this?'

I nodded. She leaned forward to look in the mirror, brushing her lashes upwards, her mouth open. 'Still,' she said, 'I wouldn't be without men. Be no fun.'

'Oh, yes. Got to have them around,' I agreed. We always had to sound nonchalant and sophisticated, even when we were alone together. 'I just think they're a terrible threat if you start to take them seriously, that's all. If life was golf, men would be bunkers.'

Liz laughed. 'How can I make my eyes look bigger?' she said.

'Draw radiating lines all round them,' I told her. 'Right up to your eyebrows as if you had inch-long lashes.' I still felt fraught. That was the word Liz and I used for the screwed-up feeling of nameless anxiety which seemed to happen so often that summer. I pulled my kimono sash tighter and said, 'I'm going to put a record on.'

At the same jumble sale where I had found my kimono, I had bought an ancient wind-up gramophone and a stack of old seventy-eight records. Most of them were rubbish but there were one or two which we played again and again.

'Let's have "Goodbye, Summer",' said Liz, busy drawing lines round her eyes with a kohl stick. I hadn't meant it seriously about the spikes but Liz would do anything. That's what I liked about her. But I frowned. 'Is this moment serious enough?' I asked. Of all the good records, the jazz and the wonderful old tangos, the one she mentioned was the most special and we had agreed only to play it in moments of great emotional significance.

'Yes,' said Liz into the mirror. 'You have made' – she turned to look at me – 'a policy statement about men being bunkers. And anyway, you're in a high state of fraughtness.' She looked amazing, as if she'd just had an electric shock and stuck like it. I wound the gramophone up and put the record on.

The orchestral introduction was ludicrous. The first time we played it I said it sounded like the horns of Elfland faintly farting, and Liz had laughed a lot. But the voice stopped us laughing. It was clear and sweet and seemed to come from miles away, and the words were so sad. I suppose the Victorians were rather obsessed with death and parting, but there was something about this song which made our skins crawl. 'All our tomorrows shall be as today,' sang the long-dead, remote soprano voice belonging to some woman called Amelita Galli-Curci. It was as if the music came back from the grave. And then the refrain. 'Goodbye, summer, goodbye, goodbye . . .' It made me shudder with an intense feeling which was hardly more pleasure than pain.

When the record was over I took it off and slipped it back in its brown paper cover, and closed the gramophone's lid. I leaned against the dressing-table with my arms folded.

'What you staring at?' asked Liz.

'Was I?' I shook my head, where the song still echoed. 'It's funny about music,' I said. 'When I listen to something marvellous, it makes me feel as if I'm bigger than my real self. As if there's a sort of huge truth somewhere, and I'm part of it, if I could only get to it A great, aching, stretching feeling.' Liz nodded. 'School's the opposite,' I went on. 'They manage to narrow everything down and chop it up into little bits. There's never anything big at school – it's all fuss about tiny details.'

'Should've left, like me,' said Liz. She frowned into the mirror. 'What if I put some silver between the black lines?'

'You'd look like a zebra crossing,' I said.

'Oh, ta,' said Liz. 'Lot of help you are. It's all right for you. You've got great big eyes anyway. Mine are like my teddy bear's eyes I had when I was a kid. His proper ones fell out so Mum sewed buttons on instead. Little pale blue buttons with faded orange fur all round.'

'Better than being born with mouse-coloured hair,' I said.

Liz grinned her uneven grin. ' 'Tisn't mouse-coloured now,' she said. 'Is it dry yet?'

I felt my head carefully and said, 'I think so. Shall I undo one and see? It ought to be sort of loose corkscrews. That's why it has to be rags and not rollers or anything.' I was picking at a knotted rag. It was going to be a frightful job disentangling them.

11

Liz turned away from the mirror and pushed her sleeves up. Her arms were plump and freckled. 'Come on,' she said. 'Lacey to the rescue.'

'Thanks,' I said. It was lovely, having someone fiddling with your hair. Liz lit another joss stick to replace one which had burned out, then set about my rags. 'It's curly all right,' she said.

It looked great. 'If I had lots of money I'd go to the hairdresser's every day,' I said.

'You didn't say what you thought about my idea,' said Liz.

'What idea?'

'Going on holiday. You mentioning money reminded me. If you get a job and save like mad, you'll have enough in a month. We could hitch-hike to somewhere hot and camp. Hey – keep still.'

'Do you think I *could* earn enough?' I suddenly felt excited. 'I'd have to tell the parents I'm not coming to Aldeburgh. Mr Mangle hasn't got any jobs at your restaurant, has he?'

'Mandel,' corrected Liz. 'No, he hasn't. There was a vacancy for a pastry chef but they've just taken a new chap on. He's super, actually – he's called Federico. Black side-burns and sleepy eyes.'

'They wouldn't have had me as a pastry chef anyway,' I said.

'No,' Liz agreed. 'You'll have to try the Job Centre tomorrow. They're shut on Sundays or we could have a look this afternoon. Not that they've ever got much.'

'I must find something better than a petrol attendant,' I said. 'That job at Easter didn't pay enough.' I was more and more excited about this new idea. 'Isn't it funny,' I said, 'ever since we played the record I feel better. That song does something to me. It's as if my clock gets stuck and the song sort of frees it.'

Liz pulled another scrap of rag out of my hair and said, 'Thank God for that. What on earth will we do when the record wears out?'

'I don't know,' I said. It made me cold to think about it.

'I really don't know.' I looked at my curly pink hair in the mirror, and smiled, because everything seemed all right again. For the time being, anyway.

Chapter 2

I had five 'O' Levels and three CSEs but it didn't help. The few cards on the boards in the Job Centre were for welders or panel-beaters or qualified nurses. I could have been an early morning cleaner, but it was only for ten hours a week and it didn't pay enough. I went over to the desk and said, 'Excuse me.'

There were three women talking among themselves but they all stopped when they noticed my hair and one of them said faintly, 'My God.' I thought it looked terrific. I had tied my purple and silver Indian scarf round it, entwined with wooden beads, and I wore my black cotton dress with a fringed shawl round the waist, and high-heeled boots. The only trouble was, it was turning out to be a hot day.

The bravest woman took a step towards me with her hand on the neck of her turquoise Crimplene dress as if in self-defence. 'Yes?' she said.

I told her I wanted a job.

'Yes,' she said again. 'What did you think you could do?'

'I *did* think I could work,' I said. She didn't have to use the past tense like that, as if I'd already been disposed of.

'Have you any experience?' she asked.

Experience. She was speaking of life's richness, my big enthusiasm. 'I've been a petrol pump attendant,' I said. 'But you can't get much experience while you're still at school, can you?'

The woman was patient, I'll say that for her. 'Have you left school now?' she enquired.

'No,' I said. 'But I need a job for the holidays.'

Mistake. She pursed her lips and shook her head with her eyes shut. Then she opened them and said with a sigh, 'People can't get permanent jobs, dear, let alone temporary ones.' She

14

glanced round rather furtively and I thought she was going to say, 'Psst!' behind her hand. Actually, she leaned her elbow on the desk and said, 'If I were you, dear, I should put a card in your local shop offering your services as a cleaner. Women who want domestic help don't come to us, you see, not with the stamp and all that. I shouldn't say so, really, but that's your best chance.' Then she looked me up and down and added, 'And if you'll take my advice, dear, you'll try to look a bit more – well – practical.'

I smiled at her. After all, she meant well. Then I picked up my gold parachute bag and walked out. Rage was storming up inside me but I told myself firmly that she couldn't help it. Being narrow-minded, fat, tasteless, ugly, incompetent, stupid, sexless and indistinguishable from a million other awful women wasn't her fault. But by the time I reached the door I was shaking with fury.

It was all such a put-down. And what would Dad say if I told him I was a domestic help? 'I'll not have it known my daughter is going out charring!' His Yorkshire accent was always more pronounced when he got upset. I knew he thought the world of me, in his funny way. And Mum. Oh, God. What a Heaven-sent opportunity to trot out her piece about there being plenty of housework to do in this house, thank-you-very-much.

The street was already hot although it wasn't much past nine o'clock. Mum had said her bit about that, too. 'Up already? Good Heavens – are you feeling all right?'

'Actually, I'm going to get a job.'

'Not with hair like that, you're not.'

'Zandra Rhodes has had her hair pink for ages, and she's one of the best designers in the world.'

'She's not looking for a job, then, is she? I don't see why you want a job, anyway.' And so on. A depressing conversation.

I didn't know where to go. Walking slowly past the shops, I felt horribly self-conscious, as I always did when I was out alone. It was fine when Liz was with me; together, we always had a purpose, even if it was only talking or laughing or walking up the street. On my own, the act fell apart. It was all right if I really was shopping or going to school, but this morning I wasn't doing anything and I suddenly felt a kind of panic. Hours of time stretched ahead and I had no idea how to fill them. The street seemed to have shrunk. When I ran along these pavements on school mornings I couldn't go fast enough to cover the exasperating distance between our house and the bus stop. This morning, a slow dawdle seemed to cover the same ground in half the time. What was I going to do? I couldn't go home and face my mother's triumph at my failure.

I went into the big department store where the perfumed air hung like a mauve curtain inside the open doors. You could waste a lot of time in a big shop. I wandered past the counters with their piles of plastic-wrapped woollies and stared at the racks of awful dresses, pale blue and salmon and apple green, uninspired, non-committal, inoffensive. My panic deepened. If I didn't watch out, I might end up in the kind of life where an expedition to a shop like this would be a big thrill. If I was a good girl, my husband would buy me a size fourteen rayon-and-polyester dress in beige or mauve on a Saturday afternoon. In flight from the dresses I found myself in Children's Wear, where a pregnant girl with a toddler writhing irritably in a push-chair fingered a romper suit. Her face was pasty and impassive, and the romper suit had a duck embroidered on the front.

Why should I expect things to be different, Mum had said. What was so special about me? All our tomorrows shall be as today. The shop was a smooth, carpeted nightmare. I took to my heels and fled. It must have looked funny, with the purple scarf flying out behind me and the beads bobbing up and down, but I didn't care. I just had to get out of that shop.

Outside on the pavement it was worse. The implacable question was waiting – well, what do you do now? I walked along towards the Underground station briskly, trying to look as if I was going somewhere. If only Liz had been with me – but Liz was sticking cherries on trifles or whatever it was she did. Sometimes I hated that restaurant she worked at.

I decided to get on the Underground and go a couple of stations up the line. There would be another Job Centre there, probably with just as few jobs, but at least I knew now that I mustn't admit that I was going back to school. I had to apply for a permanent job even if I didn't intend to keep it. I glanced at my reflection in a shoe shop window, just to make sure nothing had come adrift in my flight from the department store – and stopped dead. There was a small sheet of paper Sellotaped to the inside of the glass. I looked more closely. It said, 'Assistant wanted'. What luck! They could only have put it in that morning or dozens of people would have been after it. Perhaps there was a queue of applicants inside the shop. I went in.

There was nobody in sight except a woman in a tight skirt and a frilly blouse dusting a row of plastic-seated chairs. She finished the row before she looked up. I could see she didn't like my hair, but I didn't like hers, either. It was blue, springing rigidly from a centre parting. She looked as if she was wearing a large blue meringue. 'Can I help you?' she asked. I told her I'd come about the job and she looked away with a faint lift of her pencilled eyebrows. Sociology, question one, I thought. Define the significance of blue hair as opposed to pink hair.

'I rather think Mr Biggs has somebody in mind,' the woman said primly.

I said, 'I dare say he has.' Suddenly I thought of the thriller writer and his twice-daily women. Did Mr Biggs ravish virgins behind the Oxford Brogues? I pulled myself together and asked, 'Who is Mr Biggs?'

'The Manager,' said the woman, as if speaking of God.

'Perhaps you could ask him,' I said. 'I mean, there *is* a card in the window.'

'I don't think I need trouble him,' she said, chin held up like the Queen Mother. 'You are not experienced, are you?'

I began to feel cross. 'It doesn't say, "*Experienced* assistant",' I pointed out. 'And I've got five 'O' Levels and three CSEs.'

'Yes. Well, I will mention it to him. Perhaps you could call

17

back later?' She smiled dismissively. I decided her hair was a wig. And I knew she'd say the job was gone when I came back, whether it was or not.

'No, I couldn't,' I said. 'I want to see this Mr Bigg.'

'Biggs.'

'Well, whoever he is, I want to see him.' I knew I sounded as if I was making a scene, but I didn't care. A thin man with wispy hair came out of the door behind the counter. He took off his spectacles and blinked irritably, and said, 'Is there some trouble, Mrs Marshall?'

She said, 'Not at all, Mr Biggs,' in such a fawning voice that I thought she was going to roll on the carpet at his feet like a spaniel. 'I have already explained to this young woman,' she went on, 'that you have somebody in mind for the vacancy.'

He looked confused, obviously not understanding what he was supposed to say. I smiled at him radiantly before he came to his senses and said, 'I saw your notice in the window and I'm applying for the job. I'm very well qualified. And you need somebody young, don't you? I know lots of young people come in this shop. All my friends do!' I kept smiling and looking at him so he couldn't pay much attention to Mrs Meringue's semaphore signals behind me.

'Well –' He was flustered, torn between the old dragon and me. He couldn't stop looking at my hair. I was still smiling. 'I suppose you have a point about the young people,' he said. 'We do get quite a lot of them, specially on Saturdays . . .' His voice trailed away.

'It's such a lovely shop!' I gushed. 'I've bought ever so many pairs of shoes here!' I was glad now that Liz wasn't with me. She would never have kept a straight face.

'Would you regard this job as permanent?' Mr Biggs asked suddenly – but I was ready for that one.

'Oh, yes,' I said earnestly. 'I've always been interested in shoes. I'd like to design them really, but you have to be realistic, don't you?'

That did it. He gave in. 'All right, Miss – er?'

'Bowman,' I said. 'Sasha Bowman.'

18

'Miss Bowman. I'll give you a week's trial and we'll see how we all get on. All right, Mrs Marshall?'

Mrs Marshall sniffed and said, 'It's not up to me to decide.' Quite clearly, if it had been up to her, she would have decided otherwise.

'Right,' said Mr Biggs bravely. 'Now – er – Sasha, was it? When would you like to start?'

I decided to push my luck. 'Since it's Monday morning,' I said, 'could I start now? I've just left school, you see, and I really do need a job.'

He put his glasses on and took them off again, then said, 'Well, why not? Mrs Marshall can show you the ropes, then if you come into the office I'll get you to fill in a form and take all your particulars. And – welcome aboard!' There ought to have been a ten-gun salute or at least a bosun's whistle, but we just shook hands. I felt a bit ashamed of all my lies. I had never bought a pair of shoes here and didn't want to design the beastly things. It was a horrible shop and I had no intention of staying there any longer than it took to earn my holiday money. But you had to be tough these days. There were only jobs for people who could fight their way into them.

I felt sorry for Mr Biggs. He looked about fifty and his shoulders drooped, and he was condemned to the shoe trade for the rest of his working life. Why on earth did he do it? He gave me a little smile and I said, 'The first thing I'm going to do is take that card out of the window. I don't want anyone else coming in here after my job!' He liked that. He said, 'That's the spirit!' Then he went back to his office, but I noticed that he avoided Mrs Marshall's eye.

Mum was fretful. I think she was surprised that I'd managed to get a job, and she obviously wasn't pleased about it. She cut the end off a cauliflower and said without looking at me, 'What do you have to do at this shoe shop?'

'Sell shoes,' I said. She made an explosive noise and I wondered again why I always had to send her up. It wasn't as if I didn't know. I just couldn't resist it. 'No, actually,' I said quickly, 'I've been sticking price labels on new stock mostly, and dusting the shelves. Monday isn't a very busy day.'

'I don't see why you have to rush out and get a job,' she said. 'Can't you bear to be in the house for two minutes?'

I nearly said, no, I couldn't. Then I remembered about telling her I wasn't going to Aldeburgh. It was going to be difficult enough without upsetting her about something else. 'It isn't that,' I said.

Mum started her litany of complaint. 'When you come in from school you go up to your room or you're out hanging round that restaurant waiting for Liz Lacey. And she comes here every Sunday. I never see anything of you.'

'I know you don't like Liz,' I said, 'but I can't choose my friends to please you.' It was a silly thing to say, but it was easier than tackling the subject of Aldeburgh.

'That's obvious.' She pushed a strand of mousy hair back. I did wish she would cut it or perm it or something. It must have been pretty when it was blonde but it wasn't any more and it just made her look like a very old little girl.

Trying to brighten things up, I said, 'Shall I make some tea?'

'Suit yourself,' she said. And I lost my temper. 'Oh, *be* like that!' I shouted. 'Do you *wonder* I don't want to spend much time with you? What's the point? If I'm here it doesn't make you happy.'

She drooped. Groping, she pulled a chair out from the table and sat down, leaning her forehead in her hands. A tear dropped on the plastic surface of the table. I clenched my fists. The kitchen suddenly seemed unbearably hot. What's the matter with me, I wondered as I always did, this is my mother. She is unhappy. She is crying. I put my arm round her shoulders, feeling awkward. 'I'm sorry, Mum,' I said. 'I didn't mean to upset you, honestly.' But she was so *easily* upset. She fished in her apron pocket and I gave her a tissue from the box on the dresser. 'You don't know what it's like,' she said. 'Just going on from day to day, nobody caring if you live or die.'

I said, 'Of course we care.' I had this terrible feeling of wanting to shake her. I tried to explain. 'You seem to turn

20

everything aside,' I said. 'Nothing is ever good enough. I mean, I offered to make some tea and you just said, "Suit yourself". I was only trying to help.' It was silly to have let that annoy me so much.

'But supper's nearly ready,' she wailed. 'I've been standing here grating cheese. I don't drink tea at this time of day. Your father will be in at any minute.'

And he doesn't like cauliflower cheese, I thought. It was all so stupid. But then she said, 'Just because you've gone and got yourself a job, you think you can walk in and demand cups of tea like a miner thinks his wife will scrub his back.'

'They 'ave pit'ead baths now, moother,' I said like an idiot. She gave me a tragic red-eyed look and said on a long sigh, 'You deliberately misunderstand me, don't you.'

It was the last straw. 'Sometimes,' I said brutally, 'I think you're nuts.' I ran out of the kitchen and slammed the door, and ran up the stairs and slammed my bedroom door. I flung myself down on the bed. My feet were throbbing in their high-heeled boots and in a few minutes I sat up and took them off. I pulled the scarf and beads off my hair and undid the shawl from round my waist, then lay down again. I'd never thought that ghastly people like Mrs Marshall did a hard day's work, but I felt very tired. Tears burned behind my eyelids as I lay there with my eyes shut. My mother made me feel completely hopeless.

I was quite small the first time I saw her cry. I came into the kitchen with a snail clutched in my hand. I'd been watching it in the garden under the nasturtiums, putting its horns in and out, then I'd brought it in to show her. I climbed on a chair beside the kitchen table, with the snail held in the air and, being awkward, I knocked over a jug with my elbow. I remember the stream of milk running across the table. And Mum sat down and wept as though it was the final, unbearable blow. 'I was saving the top of the milk to go with the gooseberries,' she said. I was shattered. It seemed such a simple, well-meaning little effort and I had destroyed it. Since then I'd seen her weep on many occasions and it used to make me feel wretched. In time I learned to raise defences against the

21

misery she caused me and I watched her with a kind of anger. I think she started to hate me then, for not loving her enough. She said I was hard-boiled and selfish and I wondered if she was right. I was not sure of anything.

The front gate clicked. Dad coming home. He could never be bothered to get his key out for the front door, so he went down the side path to the back. Better go downstairs. I took off my black dress and petticoat and put my kimono on. It was lovely to be cool. I thought about what to wear the next day. Certainly something thinner. It would be a laugh to turn up in a frilly blouse and tight skirt just like Mrs Marshall. Then I knew it wouldn't be a laugh at all. She would simply think I was trying to look respectable. I went downstairs.

Dad said, 'Hello, love.' He had taken off his jacket and his waistcoat hung open like a cowboy's. He was sitting on a chair by the kitchen window with his hands lying slack on his City-suited thighs. 'Hot, isn't it?' he said. Poor Dad. He came home looking such a wreck in the hot weather but when he set out in the mornings he looked all stiff and smart. His face was rosy with the heat and his grey hair sprang up bushily from round his bald patch.

'It's boiling,' I said. 'I've been working in a shoe shop all day.'

Mum strained the cauliflower into the sink through a colander, averting her face from the cloud of steam. Dad looked at her as if expecting some comment on my job, but she frowned into the sink as if she and the cauliflower shared some bitter secret.

Dad looked back at me. 'How long are you going to do that, then?' he asked.

I admitted that I'd told them I was permanent although I really only wanted the job for a few weeks, and almost went straight on to tell him I wouldn't be coming to Aldeburgh – but the atmosphere coming from Mum paralysed me.

Dad ran his finger round his collar. 'Look,' he said, 'if you're short of money, love ... I mean, you don't *have* to work, you know.'

Mum glanced up as if she was going to say something, then

22

gave a shrug and dumped the cauliflower in a dish. She poured the cheese sauce over it from slightly too great a height. I could see splashes of the stuff plopping all over the place.

I shook my head. It still felt funny, the way my pink ringlets flew about when I did that. 'It's sweet of you,' I said to Dad, 'but I don't want to be given money. It makes me feel as if I'm not a proper person. It's bad enough still being at school.'

'That's all the thanks we get,' said Mum loudly. She banged the cauliflower cheese down on the mat in the centre of the table and snatched her apron off. Her hands were shaking. 'Help yourselves,' she said in the same loud, aggressive voice. 'I'm not hungry.' She went out and banged the door.

Dad got up and washed his hands at the kitchen sink. Drying them, he said, 'She doesn't like your hair.'

'She doesn't like *me*, as far as I can see,' I said.

He shook his head, hanging up the towel, and said, 'She loves you. But she's not seen much of the world, you know. She likes to keep things safe. Within her own little circle. And of course' – he pulled his chair out from the table, not looking at me – 'it's a difficult time for a woman, you know. At her age.' He stared at the cauliflower cheese without enthusiasm. 'We'd better eat a bit,' he said, 'or she'll be upset.'

I couldn't imagine how he could be so unemotional. Did people simply stop feeling anything when they got older, in the same way that their skins wrinkled like plums turning into prunes? Had my father ever felt as I did, or was he in some way fundamentally different? He sat down at the table and held out his plate. 'Will you do the honours?' he said.

When I had served us both I sat down and started chattering on about how silly I thought it was that females functioned in the way they did. 'Just when you most need your parents to behave like rational people,' I said, 'your mother is struck down with the menopause and turns into a weeping heap of self-pity. But what can you expect of someone who's been nothing but a wife and mother all her life? She must feel completely without purpose.'

Dad unfolded his paper and propped it against the loaf. Perhaps he felt that what I was saying was a criticism of him as a father and husband. Anyway, I shut up. Sometimes Dad and I got on really well and other times, like tonight, he just didn't want to talk. I understood, in a way. But I did feel a bit hurt about it, specially as I knew he'd read every word of that paper on the train.

Chapter 3

The shop was terribly boring. There was nobody to talk to and nothing to do, but when Mrs Marshall found me reading *Cosmo* behind the cash desk she said, 'A shop assistant's first duty, Miss Bowman, is to be ready to serve the customers. You should be on your feet, looking willing and interested.'

You didn't look very willing and interested the first day I came in here, I thought. I said, 'But there aren't any customers.'

'There may be at any minute,' she said ominously. 'And you never know that one of them is not a Divisional Inspector.'

I laughed. 'Oh, I'd spot him a mile off,' I said.

Mrs Marshall tightened her lips so that only a thin line of ruby lipstick remained visible. 'You will put that magazine away at once, Miss Bowman,' she said 'And don't let me catch you reading it again.'

'No, miss,' I said to her retreating back, and dropped a little curtsey. I did hate that woman.

To pass the time, I used to watch the people walking along the pavement outside. I could do this quite easily while pretending to rearrange the rows of beach shoes on the rack by the door. It was a kind of sport, wondering if one of the passers-by would come into the shop, almost as though I was a sea anemone trying to entice a small fish within reach of my tentacles. Not that it was very thrilling when they did come in. Since the shelves were stocked with a single shoe of every style and size, the customers seldom needed any assistance. When they had decided what they wanted they asked for the other shoe of the pair, tried them both on and, if satisfied, paid for them. All I had to do was take the money, put the shoes in a bag for the punter (as Liz always called customers) and fill any gaps in the shelves with replacement stock. Women who brought children in often wanted some help in fitting, but old ladies were the best. They never made any attempt to choose their own shoes. They just sat down and expected me to bring them endless offerings until they found something they liked or, more often, went out without buying anything. Their feet were usually horrible, lumpy and misshapen, but it was better to run about with dozens of impossible shoes than to do nothing, trying not to watch the maddeningly slow clock.

It got busier towards the end of the week and on my first Saturday it was crowded. Girls came in, almost always in twos, to pose and giggle in front of the mirrors. It was funny how I despised them although I had spent hours doing the same thing myself. Then there were wives with bored husbands and whole families with perspiring fathers. Teenagers came in gangs, men on their own. 'Handbag customers to me, Miss Bowman,' Mrs Marshall said importantly. 'The bags are chained, as you see, and the key is held by senior staff.'

I grinned and said, 'Okay.' Who would want to buy the hideous handbags, anyway? And I had quite enough to do as it was. At one point there was actually a small queue at the cash desk and when it was time for my lunch break at half-past twelve I felt for once that I'd earned it.

There would have been time to go home in the hour they allowed me for lunch, and Mum moaned because I stayed out. But that precious hour in the middle of the day was too good to waste in walking all the way home and all the way back again, specially as I knew she would make me feel guilty for putting her to the trouble of cooking, even though she wanted me to be there. So I had a sandwich in the park, and drank Coke out of a can and ate an apple and threw the core to the ducks. Being able to call myself a working girl made such a difference. There was no problem about how to spend an hour. In fact, I started to envy the leisure of people who didn't have to go back to work, even though I knew that if we changed places, that self-same leisure would fill me with panic. There was a smug virtue in glancing at my watch and thinking, another five minutes and I'll have to go. The self-respect was almost worth the long hours of boredom.

That Saturday afternoon Liz came into the shop as she had done several times during the week. Afternoons were her slack time, between lunch and the start of preparations for dinner in the evening. She perched on the edge of an Offer Bin of flip-flaps and said, 'Rushed off your feet, are you?'

'I am, actually,' I said. 'These rope-soled deck shoes are going like hot cakes.'

Liz fanned herself and said, 'Don't talk to me about hot cakes.' Her freckled face shone and her hands looked pink and puffy. 'I've been making potato croquettes all morning,' she said.

Mrs Marshall came up to push an unwanted navy blue court shoe back in the rack. She glared at Liz, who was wearing white kitchen trousers and a man's shirt with the sleeves rolled up, and said to me, 'This is hardly the time to entertain your friends, Miss Bowman.'

Liz drooped her pale eyelashes. She could look quite condescending when she chose. 'Just imagine I'm a punter,' she said to Mrs Marshall. 'Then you'll feel better.'

I thought Mrs Marshall was going to burst. You could see her swelling with outrage. 'I would remind you, Miss Bowman,' she said, 'that you are here on a week's trial. Mr Biggs is very much influenced by my opinion in these matters.'

It was then, while the three of us were standing in a silly group, that the boy in a leather jacket pushed past. He had a yellow crash helmet looped over his arm and he said, 'When you lot finish nattering, I might be able to buy some shoes.' He stared at the trainers with his hands in his pockets.

Mrs Marshall said, 'Don't just stand there, Miss Bowman – serve the customer.' And she stalked off.

'What a cow,' said Liz cheerfully. 'I better get out of your hair before you get the sack.'

'You working tonight?' I asked her, and she nodded. 'Got the afternoon off till five then I'm on until we close. See you tomorrow.'

'Okay. See you.'

27

Liz jumped off the bin and went out. I could see Mrs Marshall frowning at me from behind the cash register so I went over to see what the boy who had pushed past us wanted. He was turning over an Addidas trainer in his big, dirty hands, and I thought he looked as suspicious as a chimpanzee I saw once at the Zoo, inspecting an empty beer can. 'They got gold laces or something?' he asked. 'Hell of a price, isn't it?'

I said we'd got some other ones, and showed him. He wasn't too pleased with those, either. 'Load of rubbish,' he said. 'Bloody cardboard.'

I could see he was going to be difficult. 'What about basketball boots?' I suggested. 'Lots of people buy those.'

He lounged against the rack and folded his arms. The yellow crash-helmet stuck out from his elbow, taking up a lot of room. His hair was dark and tousled and he looked bored. I thought he was a real hard case. 'Go on, then,' he said. 'Show me what you got.'

I very nearly told him to go and look for himself. The place was now crammed with other customers and Mrs Marshall was ringing up purchases like a robot gone mad. Poor old Mr Biggs was trying to sell sandals to a huge family complete with a screaming baby. But Mrs Marshall glared at me again so I trotted round to the basketball boots like a good girl and came back with an armful. 'These are the most expensive ones, but they've got really good padding round the ankles,' I told him. 'Then there's these Union Jack ones, or the yellow and black –' I wondered why I was bothering. He wasn't going to buy any shoes. He was just idling some time away. I had done it so often myself that I could spot it a mile off.

'Might as well try something on,' he said, and he slumped down on a chair and flung his foot up on a footstool. He didn't make any attempt to undo the laces of his grubby plimsolls.

I said, 'What size do you take?'

He shrugged. 'Dunno.' I looked at him, trying to keep my temper. Under his leather jacket he wore a white shirt without a collar, unironed and crumpled, but a lovely quality poplin, the sort of thing I'd have bought if I'd seen it in a junk shop. And he had a red cotton scarf knotted round his neck. He knew I was getting cross. He grinned and said, 'Aren't you going to measure my feet, then?' I took a measuring stick from under the footstool and tugged at the laces of his beastly plimsoll.

'They used to have those machines when I was a kid,' he said. 'You stood in a sort of hole and the sides slid in, front to back and side to side.' He demonstrated with his hands. 'Zerp – zerp. Then the numbers came up on a little green video. Don't you have one of them?'

'No, we don't,' I snapped. 'You want a size eleven.'

'See what you can find, then, darling,' he said. He pulled a tin of tobacco and a packet of papers from his pocket and began to make himself a cigarette.

I came back with another armful of shoes. 'There's this one,' I said patiently, 'or this – but we've only got the Union Jack basketball boots in your size. Or you could have a pair of tennis shoes.'

He leaned back as if he was a Roman emperor and flicked ash on the carpet from his skinny little cigarette. 'Wouldn't be seen dead in Union Jacks,' he said. 'And them Addidas is too much bread. I'll try the trainers.'

I said, 'You can try those on while I see to someone else, can't you? There's a lot of people waiting.'

He shook his head. 'Don't give me that, darling,' he said. 'Like a woman at the hairdresser's, innit? Come in for a bit of pampering. Spot of the old grovel. Got your little shoe horn, have you?'

Suddenly I blew up. I jumped to my feet, absolutely blazing with fury. 'I'm not grovelling to you or anyone else,' I shouted at him. 'You didn't come in here to buy any shoes, you came to muck me about. Well, you can just piss off and try it on someone else, because as far as I'm concerned, it's just *not on*!'

Everyone was staring. Mrs Marshall came rushing up and said, 'That is quite enough, Miss Bowman!' Mr Biggs was behind her, looking more flustered than ever. 'What on earth

29

is going on?' he asked.

It was Mrs Marshall's moment of triumph. She raised her thin eyebrows at him and said, 'I think you will agree, Mr Biggs, that Miss Bowman's trial period has *not* been satisfactory!' And she stalked off to the cash desk. I had played right into her hands. I was so angry that I almost wept. 'I don't care,' I said obstinately. 'There's some things I just won't put up with.'

The boy had put both feet on the footstool. He was sitting back comfortably with his arms folded and his ankles crossed, and his cigarette stuck out of his mouth at a jaunty angle. He was thoroughly enjoying the scene he had caused. 'That woman's a right old bat,' he told Mr Biggs conversationally, jerking his head in the direction of Mrs Marshall. 'You want to get rid of her, to start with.' He grinned and added, 'This popsy with the candyfloss hair's all right. Just wants to learn a bit of proper respect, that's all.' I looked at him with hatred. He wiggled the toes of his shoeless foot luxuriously. There was a large hole in his sock.

I wanted to keep my job. I knew I had been amazingly lucky to get it, and in any case, the thought of telling Mum I'd got the sack was a nightmare. Usually when I lost my temper I would say anything that came into my head but this time I knew I had to retrieve the situation. I turned to Mr Biggs and looked up at him piteously. 'I didn't think working in a shoe shop would be like this,' I said, doing my damsel in distress act. 'I thought it was a – a *decent* job.'

He couldn't resist it. He straightened his drooping shoulders and stared sternly down at the boy. 'There is no reason why my assistants should be subjected to any harassment,' he said sternly. 'I must ask you to leave the shop.'

The boy grinned. 'All right, Dad,' he said cheerfully. He waved his cigarette at the bronze pedestal ashtray which stood just out of his reach and said, 'Ashtray.' I would have told him to get it himself, but poor Mr Biggs was trained to comply with the customer's wishes. He moved the ashtray within reach. The boy nipped off the glowing end of his cigarette between finger and thumb then took out his tobacco tin and put the remains of the cigarette into it. He replaced the tin in his pocket and said, 'Who's going to put my shoe on for me?' But that was going too far. 'Nobody,' he said. 'Thought not.' He was completely unconcerned. He pushed his foot into its plimsoll and tied the lace quickly. Then he picked up his crash-helmet and got to his feet. ''Bye, Dad,' he said to Mr Biggs. 'You can go home proud today. You did your bit for the Empire.' He winked at me. ''Bye, darling. See you around.'

And suddenly I almost giggled. He wandered out, stopping to gaze at some gold evening sandals by the door as if he found them really interesting.

I fell to my knees and stared gathering up shoes, gazing up at Mr Biggs appealingly. 'I won't lose my job, will I?' I asked him. 'I'm sorry I was rude but – you should have heard what he said.' I looked away modestly, managing to blush.

Mr Biggs was such a nice man, really. He said, 'Of course you won't lose your job, my dear. We mustn't kow-tow to these yobboes.' He gave a little tug at the front of his jacket and straightened his shoulders again. He was having a good day. He even looked Mrs Marshall straight in the eye, causing her to turn away huffily. Then he marched across the carpeted floor to a massively fat, perspiring woman whose feet sprouted bunions the size of golf balls, splitting the uppers of her ancient slippers from their soles. 'Yes, madam,' he said confidently, waving her to a chair. 'Do sit down. I'm sure we can help you.' I wished him luck.

Liz was quite envious when I told her about the scene with the boy in a leather jacket. 'I wish I'd stayed,' she said. 'Fancy Mr Biggs actually passing him the ashtray! Honestly, some people have got no self-respect. Federico's like that. He grovels round the punters like a walking doormat. Mind you, what he says about them in the still room is nobody's business.'

I wound the gramophone up and put on a Louis Armstrong record called, 'It's Sleepy Time Down South'. Through the rasping of the battered surface, the lazy trumpet notes dropped into the sunny morning like cool water. After being shut in that stuffy shop all week I didn't want the curtains drawn today. Things seemed different. Even the sunshine was different, as if I had never noticed it before. I said, 'I keep thinking about him.'

'Who?' asked Liz. 'Mr Biggs?' She was stupid sometimes.

'No, the bloke in a leather jacket,' I said. 'Just when he was going out, I suddenly thought it was all rather funny, He was only in the place for about ten minutes, and caused absolute bedlam.'

'Big deal,' said Liz. She stared at herself in the mirror and said, 'I think I'll get my hair cut really short.'

'If you do that, you want to dye it proper carrots,' I said. 'Otherwise you'll look like a camel.'

'Oh, ta,' said Liz. 'Honesty Bowman strikes again. I don't know why I'm friends with you sometimes. What d'you mean, you keep thinking about him?'

I didn't know whether I wanted to talk about it or not. There was no way I could express what I felt without sounding silly. I went and looked out of the window. My father was mowing the lawn 'He just keeps coming back into my mind,' I said. 'I wish I hadn't made such a fuss. He'll think I was really up-tight.'

Liz stared at me. 'What does it matter what he thinks?' she said. 'He's just some bloke who was giving you the run-around, isn't he?'

'Yes,' I said. Dad reached the end of the lawn and turned the mower round, holding the cable out carefully so he wouldn't mow over it. I thought about the boy's big hands and their surprising neatness as he spread the tobacco along the thin paper. And the red scarf knotted round his neck. I turned back to Liz and said, 'What are we going to do tonight?'

She looked down at her nails. They were purple today. She wasn't allowed to wear nail varnish at the restaurant so she always went mad with it on Sundays. I wondered why she thought it was worth it. 'Actually,' she said, 'I'm going out with Gary Weston. I bumped into him when I left your shop yesterday, and we went and had a cup of coffee.'

'Gary Weston?' I said. 'He's such a *weed*.' What was I going to do this evening without Liz?

'You haven't seen him since he left school,' said Liz. 'He's not weedy now. Well, not very.'

'What's he doing?' I asked out of politeness.

'Works in a garage.'

'Oh.'

The record trumpeted on. 'Look,' said Liz, 'I've got to see other people sometimes, you know.'

'Yes, of course,' I said quickly. And, to soothe the awkwardness between us, I added, 'We both have. I mean, it's all experience.'

This was safe ground. Experience was all-important that summer. I think we felt that the lack of it would condemn us to eternal childhood.

'Exactly,' said Liz. 'Talking about things is okay but it's not like getting out there and doing them.' Then she said, 'Have you told your parents about us going abroad?'

I felt my stomach tighten uneasily. 'No,' I said. 'Mum's been in such a bad mood this week. I thought I'd wait until she's cheered up a bit.'

'Don't leave it too long,' Liz advised. 'If they've booked somewhere, they'll have to cancel your bit and they won't get a refund if it's at the last minute.'

'Oh, Lord.' I hadn't thought of that. Suddenly it seemed as if I couldn't quite believe it. 'Liz,' I said, 'We are really going, aren't we? I mean, you won't go off with Gary or something?'

'Of course I won't,' she said crossly. She stared at herself in the mirror, pushing her pale gingery hair away from her face with both hands. 'I think I will get my hair cut, all the same,' she said. 'It's so blooming hot in that kitchen.'

I went and looked out of the window again, and the record came to an end. Liz lifted the needle and put the playing arm back in its clip. In the silence after the record's rasping crackle the whirr of the mower floated up. Big hands. Red scarf. Crumpled white cotton shirt.

Liz was looking at me. 'You haven't fallen for that bloke,

have you?' she asked. The sunlight lay across the window-sill with a new intensity; across the Indian bedcover, across the burned-out joss sticks in the little pot on the mantelpiece. 'No, of course I haven't,' I said. And that day, I still almost believed it was true.

Chapter 4

I went to work on Monday morning feeling strangely excited. I dusted the shelves and put new shoes on display to replace the ones that had been sold and then wiped all the chair seats with a damp cloth. The army of kids that came in on Saturdays left the place horribly sticky. And all the time I had half an eye on the door. Every time I turned round I thought I was going to see him looking at the trainers, with the yellow crash-helmet over his arm. Once a boy in a leather jacket walked past and my heart seemed to jump in my chest and a blush ran up my neck and spread over my face. That's when I really knew I had got involved. As the boy, who had walked past the shop, turned to glance at the window I saw that his face was spotty and he had a stupid blobby nose. I felt desperately ashamed to have mistaken him for my boy.

I went into the corner behind the desert boots to think about it. My boy. What was I talking about? He was just some casual bloke who had come into the shop to waste a bit of time. Most probably I would never see him again. Why should I? But when I said that to myself I felt as if I was trying to kill something. The excitement vanished and the light seemed to go out of the day. I turned over a desert boot in my hands and thought of his hands turning over the Addidas trainer. Never again. Never. There was a hard feeling in my throat and I wanted to sit down somewhere and cry.

Mrs Marshall looked over the top of the rack and said, 'Isn't it time you made the tea, Miss Bowman?' So I went off to the kitchen. It was a tiny room behind the shop, next to the toilet, and it smelt of stale tea leaves and gas. Mr Biggs came in. 'All right this morning, Sasha?' he enquired.

I said, 'Yes, thanks.' I couldn't think why he asked, but he went on, 'Any more trouble, my dear, and you just come

35

straight to me.' I must have looked blank because he added, 'Pestering from these young thugs, you know. You don't have to put up with it.'

I said, 'Oh, you mean any others. Yes. Thank you, Mr Biggs.' And I really did feel quite grateful to him because I hated the thought of being messed around by someone like the spotty-faced boy who had just walked past the shop.

The rest of the day was terribly empty. I went to the park at lunch time but my sandwiches seemed as unattractive as recycled cardboard and I broke them up and threw them to the ducks. I drank my can of Coke very slowly, then sat with the empty tin in my hands, looking at the people walking about under the trees. I wondered where he worked. Where he lived. Surely it must be somewhere local. Nobody would come to a grotty London suburb on a Saturday afternoon if they lived somewhere else. You would go on a shopping trip to the West End perhaps, but not to a place like this. But he had a bike. He could have been on his way to somewhere else. Or wasting time while he waited for his girl friend.

That thought hurt. I don't know why I went on following it, but I did. I imagined him smiling at a girl who came hurrying out of a smart office, putting his arm round her as they walked off together. I hated her although she didn't exist. The grass was pale in the sun. People walked about in another world. They were not me. I was as separate as a goldfish in its own bowl, looking out through the glass.

I went back to the shop when it was time, and watched the door all afternoon. It seemed to last for days and days. Mr Biggs smiled at me when I gave him his tea and said, 'Cheer up! It may never happen.' 'Probably not,' I said gloomily and almost added, 'That's just the trouble.' But I managed to give him a smile instead and he said, 'That's better.'

At last it was time to go home. I picked up my bag from the kitchen and went out, looking over my shoulder to wave at poor, kind, well-intentioned Mr Biggs. I had decided to treat him as if he was a disaster area and I was Oxfam. I was so busy smiling at him that I didn't look where I was going.

'Watch it,' said someone I almost collided with. It was him.

The boy in a leather jacket. I felt my face go so hot that I couldn't think of anything else except how annoyed I was to be blushing. 'Well, *you* watch it,' I said, stupidly.

He said, 'You didn't get the sack, then?'

'No. Mr Biggs let me stay.' Why couldn't I find something worldly-wise and amusing to say? He had been rolling himself a cigarette and he asked, 'Got a light?' I shook my head. I had always hated the smell of dirty ashtrays and Liz, hygiene-conscious because of her training in catering, said it was disgusting. But now I wished I smoked. I could have whipped a lighter out of my bag, flicked it, lit his cigarette. 'Hold that,' he said, giving me his tobacco tin. It felt warm. He patted all his pockets then fished in them, at last producing a single rather grey pink-headed match with a bit of fluff stuck to it. 'What d'you bet I can't do it,' he said, then held up one knee and raked the match along the taut denim of the underside of his jeans. It lit. I said, 'Do I clap?' and he grinned, holding the match to his thin cigarette. 'Just throw money,' he said.

We started to walk along the street together. It seemed as if I was dreaming. 'Thought I'd better come and say I'm sorry,' he said, 'mucking you about on Saturday.'

I told him it was all right. 'I thought afterwards it was quite a laugh,' I said. 'You must have thought I was a nut case, though, going off the handle like that.'

'Winding you up, wasn't I?' he admitted cheerfully. 'I'd have done the same as you, stuck up for my rights. I've lost ever so many jobs that way.'

'What sort of job have you got now?' I asked.

'I haven't,' he said. 'One of the great army, I am. I thought they'd have given you the sack. If you hadn't been there I was going to go in and make them give me your address.'

'Were you?' I said, pleased.

'Yes,' he said. We went on walking along the pavement. Then we both started to say something at once, and both stopped, and he said, 'You first.'

'What sort of job do you want?' I asked, and he said, 'Try anything. I was repairing washing machines last, but the firm went bust. I've had eighteen different jobs since I left school.

Load of rubbish, all of them.'

'But what do you *want* to do?' I asked.

He shrugged his shoulders. 'I'd *like* to be an engineer. I've got interested in developing two-strokes. People don't realise their potential. But you need a degree and I haven't even got 'A's. Left school like a rocket, soon as I could. Don't know who was more relieved, me or them. How about you? Happy in the shoe shop?'

I was appalled that he might think of me as a budding Mrs Marshall. I told him all about wanting to go to art school and be a designer and having to stay on at school and getting the job in the shoe shop so as to go on holiday with Liz, and he didn't interrupt. When I got to the end he still didn't say anything except, 'Best of luck. Hope you make it.' After a pause I said, 'What were you going to say?'

'Nothing,' he said.

'Yes, you were. When we both started together.'

'Oh. I was going to ask if you'd like a cup of coffee but –'

'I'd love one!' I said.

He grinned a bit sheepishly and said, 'Thing is, I'm down to twenty-four pence. It's only for today. I'll be down the DHSS tomorrow.'

'What's that?' I asked, and he laughed. 'Shows you never been on the dole,' he said. 'Department of Health and Social Security. Madam!'

I felt terribly ashamed. We came to a café called Ron's with a big Coca-Cola sign outside it and he pushed the door open. 'Come on,' he said. 'I don't mind you buying me a cup of coffee. I got no pride.' The back-to-back seats with tables between them were full of people but there were a couple of empty stools at the shelf which ran round the wall. He nodded at them and said, 'Park yourself,' and went to the counter. I fished in my bag but he said, 'Afterwards,' so I went and perched on a stool.

My parents would have hated Ron's. If we ever went out to eat it was usually to the Trattoria or to the Greek place my mother liked, although we hadn't done that for a long time now. And if we were on our way somewhere in the car and

38

stopped for a break Mum and Dad always chose a place with black beams, preferably leaning sideways. 'Got a spot of character,' Dad would say. Ron's had no character at all. People stubbed their cigarettes out in the saucers. Being there made me feel rather daring but I hoped it didn't show. I tried to look bored.

He came back with two cups of coffee and a couple of biscuits wrapped in silver paper and said, 'What's your name? I do like to know who I'm borrowing money from.'

'Sasha Bowman,' I said.

'Mine's Nick,' he said. 'Dominic Alexander Cartwright, to be exact.'

I didn't tell him my parents still insisted on calling me Susan. It was annoying the way they kept coming back into my mind, anyway. I did wish I lived away from home. I asked Nick where he lived.

'With my dad,' he said. 'Mum shoved off and we've got this Council flat, so I chip in with the rent and all that. You don't get a lot to chuck around when you're on the Social, though.'

I said I'd like to have a place of my own and somehow I got onto the subject of having a career and how awful I thought it was that so many girls gave everything up to get married. 'After all,' I said, 'you don't have to have a baby these days unless you want to, so what's the panic about getting married?'

'Dead right,' he agreed. 'And anyway, people change all the time. You like something one day, you don't like it the next. I can't imagine getting so hooked on just one person that I wanted to stay with them for the rest of my life.'

'Too much of a gamble, isn't it?' I said lightly. But my confident line of reasoning had led me to a cliff's edge which I had not expected and I felt a shiver of dismay. Just one person. Was I no more than that? Suddenly I knew I wanted to matter to him. My reasonable self was appalled by the idea but I didn't care. I wanted to be the one special person in Nick's life. I had got a pound note out of my purse while he was at the counter and I folded it and slipped it under his saucer. He said, 'Bit much, isn't it, meet a girl for the first time and borrow a quid off her. I'll pay you back tomorrow, honest.'

I had been paid on Friday for my first week at the shop and it was wonderful to have money of my own. And I would see Nick again tomorrow. Dominic. Such a lovely name. I smiled at him and he smiled back. 'Anyway,' he said, 'it gives me an excuse to see you again.'

'Do you need one?' I asked.

His smile faded and he put his cup back in its saucer with a curiously delicate precision. 'People aren't always as tough as they look,' he said. 'Not underneath.' Then he retreated into self-mockery. 'Nothing like a quid in the hand for self-defence. You might attack me with a shoe-horn otherwise. You ever seen that film on the telly about spiders mating? Poor chap takes his life in his hands.'

'So you'd rather take a pound note,' I agreed. And we went on talking about spiders and other things we'd seen on TV nature programmes.

'I wouldn't mind being a tiger,' I said when we found we'd both watched a programme about Bengal. I narrowed my eyes and felt tigerish. 'Claws and muscles and nobody arguing.'

'What, gobbling up poor little zebras?' said Nick, grinning. 'What have they done to deserve it?'

'Serves them right for being zebras,' I said firmly. 'Wearing coats that blend in with the background, all looking the same as each other – zebras are boring. Nearly as bad as people.'

Nick shook his head, closing his eyes for a moment so that the dark lashes made two upward curves. He was marvellous to look at. 'Nothing's as boring as people,' he said. 'Most of them bore me so much, it hurts.'

'I know what you mean,' I said. 'Being in the shop with Mrs Marshall is like rubbing on a Crimplene cheese grater all day.'

He laughed. 'Crimplene cheese grater,' he repeated. 'Dead right.'

Time went by. When at last we left the café we walked along

to where he had parked his bike and he got astride it and started it up. I had never really looked at a motor bike before. They had always seemed to be heavy, noisy things with complicated pipes and tubes all over them but now, as I looked at the long leather saddle and watched Nick's hand turning the twist grip back towards him to rev the engine with a rattling roar, there was a real personality about the bike which was almost overwhelming.

'What sort is it?' I shouted, and he shouted back, 'Honda Superdream.' He let the engine noise settle to a quieter level and asked if I had a crash helmet. I shook my head. 'I'll see if I can borrow one,' he said. 'Can't take you on the back without a bone-dome.' I felt breathless at the thought of being on the bike with him, not because it was dangerous or anything like that, but because it was something I had never imagined.

Nick said he would have to go. His father was a storeman, he said, and he liked Nick to be in the house with the kettle on when he came home from work. 'Be different if I had a job,' Nick said. 'I'd tell him to take a running jump. As it is, I suppose I'd better be there. Keep him happy.' I said I understood, and started to tell him about Mum always wanting me to be in the house, but the bike's engine was too loud and anyway, he had put his crash-helmet on and couldn't hear me very easily and I felt silly, standing there in the street talking about my mother.

'See you!' he shouted, and I nodded and waved. Then he roared off and I walked home.

The next day he came into the shop at lunchtime. I was busy cramming a child's foot into a sensible shoe which she hated but which her mother approved of, so I couldn't go and see Nick straight away. He took a little wind-up frog out of his pocket and set it hopping along the top of the cash register. Mrs Marshall's eyes bulged. She looked rather like a frog herself as she crouched on a footstool in front of an old lady. The little girl pulled her foot out of the sensible shoe and ran across in one sandal and a white sock to see what Nick was doing. He gave her the frog and said, 'You have a go. His name's Gunk.' She was delighted but her mother got up crossly and said, 'I'll leave it just now, thank you.' She gathered up her handbag and the child's other sandal and went over to her daughter saying, 'Tracey, do come *along*.'

Mr Biggs came out of his office and saw Nick. He snatched his glasses off as the woman pushed the frog crossly back at Nick and dragged her reluctant child out of the shop after making her return the frog to Nick.

'You have no right to enter this shop unless you intend to make a purchase,' said Mr Biggs. Nick grinned amiably and said, 'Keep your hair on, Dad.' He nodded across at me and said, 'Just waiting for old Lolly-top there.' Then he wound the frog up and set it off again.

Mr Biggs gave me a thunder-struck look. Then he put his glasses on firmly and started riffling through a sheaf of invoices as though they were very important. Mrs Marshall said, 'You may go to lunch, Miss Bowman. And kindly remember what I told you about – friends – coming to the shop.'

She paused on the word 'friends' as though putting it in quotes, and gave Nick a look like a blast of fly-killer. He smiled at her. 'I bet you were a beauty in your young days,' he said.

We went to the park and sat on a bench near the pond, and Nick returned the pound he had borrowed and shared my sandwiches. He started to talk about his father. It sounded awful. Mr Cartwright was a man with a violent temper. 'Like a kid,' Nick said. 'Flies into a rage if things go wrong. That's why Mum left, because he used to knock her about. Don't blame her. She's shacked up with another bloke now, in Croydon. Dad won't have a go at me, though, not now I'm bigger than him. It was different when I was a kid.' He frowned, thinking about it. Then he said, 'We had a terrible fight soon after Mum left, and I laid him out. I thought I'd killed him. Sometimes I wish I had.'

I said, 'You'd have gone to prison.' But he said he was only fifteen at the time, so he wouldn't. And anyway, he said, everyone knew about his father being so violent. Nobody

42

would have blamed him.

I felt a great ache inside me as I looked at Nick. It wasn't just that I was sorry for him – being sorry is easy and somehow rather patronising. What I felt was a sense of waste and desolation. It seemed as if I had known him always, and yet there was nothing I could do for him. I looked at his face as he talked, trying to remember everything about it so that I could recall it later, the way his untidy dark hair fell over his forehead, the thin, flat sides of his face that broke into creases when he smiled, the wide mouth with big, square teeth. And his eyes. Nick had marvellous eyes, a greeny-grey colour with dark edges to the irises. And his eyelashes were so dark that they looked as if he was wearing mascara.

That evening I tried to draw his face from memory, but it was maddeningly difficult. When I tried to visualise him I could only see little bits of his face – the eyelashes, the curling hair, the corners of his mouth. I couldn't put them together. I covered sheet after sheet of paper but gave it up at last and went back to doing fashion drawings, but even they seemed hard work.

Liz rang up when she had finished work and said, 'You got the afternoon off tomorrow?'

'Yes,' I said, 'it's early closing.'

'That's what I thought,' said Liz. 'Let's go somewhere. Down the Elephant market and look for clothes or something. What did you do on Sunday night?'

It seemed ages ago. 'Stayed in and watched telly,' I said. 'How was Gary?'

'All right,' said Liz. 'I quite like him, actually. Here – I met Maureen and she said she saw you with a bloke in a leather jacket. It wasn't that one who came in the shop, was it?'

'Yes,' I said, trying to sound casual.

'*Really?*' Liz was bursting with curiosity. 'You secretive old thing, you. Why didn't you ring me up and tell me all about it?'

I knew Mum was listening. Dad was out that night and she was in the kitchen with the door open. After a pause I said, 'Much better to wait until I see you.'

Liz understood. 'I know what you mean,' she said. 'Listen, come round to the restaurant tomorrow when you get off. You know where the back door is, don't you? Don't fall over the dustbins!'

'All right,' I said, a bit unwillingly. It wasn't that I didn't want to see Liz – in fact, I was longing to tell her all about Nick. But he didn't know it was early closing day tomorrow. That is, I hadn't specifically mentioned it. There were no plans made. But somehow I felt reluctant to commit the afternoon to something excluding Nick. Just in case.

'Sasha?' Liz said. '*Is* that all right?'

'It's fine,' I said, but she wasn't convinced. 'You don't sound as if it's fine,' she said suspiciously. Mum came out of the kitchen and I heard her pause outside the open sitting-room door. Liz said, 'What's going on? Are you still there?' I said, 'Yes, I'm here,' and waited until Mum went very slowly up the stairs. I knew what she would look like, leaning on the banister rail as if she was pulling herself up, looking terribly tired.

'See you tomorrow,' I said.

'Yeah,' said Liz. 'I get the picture. Don't let it get you down. See you.' She rang off.

I resolved to go straight upstairs and tell Mum I wouldn't be going to Aldeburgh, right now, before I chickened out of it. While Dad was out, it might be easier to tackle her on her own. Dad was out quite a lot at that time. I ran upstairs and found Mum in her bedroom. The wardrobe door was open and she was sitting on the bed with a long blue dress across her knees. She was staring at it, nibbling her thumb nail anxiously. 'That's your choir dress, isn't it?' I said. She belonged to some choir that sang awful things like *Elijah*. She nodded, not looking at me. 'I was wondering if I could let it out,' she said. 'We've got a concert next week and last time I wore it, it seemed a bit tight.' She put her hand over her eyes and shook her head. 'It's so awful, getting old,' she said.

Don't cry, I begged her silently, oh, please don't cry or I shall be angry and I don't want to be. As if she had heard me she put her hand down and her face was composed, her lips tight. 'But then,' she said, 'it's not exactly unique, is it. We all get old.' I sat down beside her and took up the dress, unzipped it and turned it inside out. 'You could release these darts,' I said. 'It doesn't look as if it's faded – they wouldn't show, not if you pressed it well. Shall I do it for you?'

'You don't want to bother with that,' she said.

'If I didn't want to bother I wouldn't have offered,' I said. 'Have you got your little sharp nail scissors?' She fetched them and I clipped the stitches. The darts had been put in the bodice and skirt before the dress had been sewn together at the waist, so I had to undo most of the waist stitching as well. After a bit she said, 'I'm sorry I've been a bit cross lately.'

'It's all right,' I said. There was an uneasy pause while I went on clipping. I could imagine my voice telling her quite calmly that I wasn't going to Aldeburgh, but I still couldn't say it. I decided to lead up to it gently. I took a deep breath then let it out again. Must sound casual. Another breath. 'Liz and I were talking the other day,' I began, 'and we thought –'

'Liz,' she interrupted on a long sigh as if I had touched on a very sore point. And, coward that I was, I let myself be side-tracked. 'Look, Mum, Liz is all right,' I said.

She looked aggrieved. 'Why couldn't you have made friends with some of those nice girls in your form at school – Diana and Geraldine and Sarah? You used to bring them to the house when you were younger, and you can't say they're not intelligent girls. They're all hoping to go to University, aren't they?'

'Oh, yes,' I said grimly. 'They'll all do the right thing.' I had never been able to explain, even to myself, why I felt so different from the nice girls at school. It was this business of clubs. Not formal clubs like the Drama Society, but the tacitly-assumed membership of a certain group, together with the proper behaviour which that group expected. None of the other A-stream girls ever used mauve lipstick or wore an Art overall so stiff with paint that it stood up on its own. I liked

45

my overall but the others thought I was showing off. Perhaps I was. But school was so boring, and the girls who belonged to the Nice Club never seemed to mind it. They weren't bored and so I despised them, though I tried not to show it. But they knew, and they waited like neat little cats for me to come prancing out of my mouse-hole. I gave as good as I got, but it was a battle, all the time. And I was sick of it. The boys thought I was mad, too, but they didn't count. They were such *kids*. The only person who was on my wave-length was Liz. She was always ready to do anything crazy and she didn't belong to the Nice Club. She belonged to a different club, and I didn't like to think about that too much, because I was stuck with being too Nice to belong to Liz's club. I didn't belong anywhere.

'I can't see what's the matter with doing the right thing,' said Mum with her chin in the air. 'But I don't suppose Liz Lacey would understand *that*.'

'Nobody has to understand it,' I said. And I nearly launched into a tirade, but I managed not to. I was getting better at controlling my temper these days. Perhaps my still-secret excitement about Nick was giving me strength. I imagined telling Mum that I had a boy friend who rode a motor bike and had a father who had beaten up his mother, and nearly laughed. I shook the dress out and said, 'There. Now put it on inside out and I'll pin it to fit, then run it up on the machine.'

'You must take after your dad's father, I think,' Mum said. 'I'm hopeless at that sort of thing. He was a tailor, you know, in Leeds.'

'Yes, I know,' I said. She pulled her cotton dress over her head and stood there in her slip, rather thick down the middle and with her arms looking white and flabby, and I felt a sudden painful sympathy for her. So, once again, I failed to tell her about Aldeburgh. Or at least, that's the excuse I made.

46

Chapter 5

It was hot again the next day. The sun blazing in the street outside the shop made me long for one o'clock when I would be free for the whole afternoon. Just as we were closing, Nick walked in and I saw at once that he had an extra crash-helmet over his arm, a white one with a black stripe across the centre. Mrs Marshall looked at him and began, 'You have already been told – '

'Come off it, darling,' Nick interrupted, smiling at her with unruffled charm. 'Only picking up the girl friend, aren't I? You coming, Lolly-top?'

'I wish you wouldn't call me Lolly-top,' I said as we went out. 'Don't you like my hair being pink?'

'I think it's great,' he said, 'won't lose you in a crowd, will I? What colour is it really?'

'Mouse,' I told him. 'Like my mother's. I wish I could have taken after Dad. He had lovely dark wavy hair when I was little. Going a bit bald now, though.'

'You don't want to take after him, then,' said Nick. 'I hate bald women. Here, try this on.' He handed me the crash helmet. I put my bag down on the pavement. 'No, not like that,' he said. 'Not on the back of your head. Chin first. Get right *into* it.'

The crash helmet felt heavy and strange. Its edges surrounded my face like a close, personal space craft. 'Do the strap up,' Nick instructed. 'It's awfully tight,' I said. 'It has to be,' he told me. 'A loose crash helmet is useless. Does more harm than good.' He tried to wriggle the helmet on my head and I said, 'Ow!' 'That's great,' he said.

'Where did you get it?' I asked. My voice sounded funny and my breath misted up the inside of the perspex visor. I pushed it up. 'Borrowed it,' said Nick. 'Friend of mine crashed his bike. Didn't damage the helmet, though.' He looked at me critically. 'Those are silly clothes for biking.' I was wearing a short ruffled skirt and a floppy blouse, and my high-heeled sandals. I pointed out I was wearing my shop-girl clothes and I hadn't expected to be biking, and he said, 'But it's early closing day.' He sounded as if I ought to have taken it for granted that I'd be going somewhere with him and instead of being annoyed about it I felt faintly guilty for not having dressed more sensibly.

'Where are we going?' I asked, and he shrugged his shoulders. 'Where you like,' he said. 'Country? Seaside? You name it.' I didn't know what to say, I started nibbling away at the alternatives with small objections, like my mother did when faced with a choice. 'It's not worth going to the seaside,' I said. 'By the time we got there it would be time to come home again.' 'Be there in an hour,' he said. But then I remembered Liz. I told him I couldn't go anywhere until I'd been to see her at the restaurant and explained what I was doing. He didn't seem too sure about that. 'She won't like you just walking up and saying you're not going out with her after all, will she?' he said when I had told him about our arrangement. 'Look, if you've promised to go out with her. I'll shove off.' I was in a panic. 'Oh, no, don't!' I said. 'She'll be all right, honest. Liz isn't like that.'

'Pretty funny girl if she's not,' he said darkly. But I thought, if Liz can go out with Gary when she wants to, I can go out with Nick. She's got no right to object. But she wouldn't anyway.

We came to the bike and he backed it off its stand and put the foot rests down. 'You been on a bike before?' he asked me. I shook my head and the crash-helmet felt as if it was trying to chew my ears off. 'Well, just sit close to me and don't try to steer,' he said. 'Keep your feet away from the exhaust pipe, it gets hot.' I said, 'What do you mean, try to steer?'

'Some pillion passengers lean the bike round corners,' he said. 'Specially if they're bike riders themselves. And if the two of you have got different ideas, you're in trouble.'

It sounded frightening. He straddled the bike and said, 'Hop on then.' I got astride it as well, and felt for the foot rests. 'All right?' he asked. 'Hang on to your bag. Don't let it dangle about.' And we were off.

It was marvellous. At first it seemed bumpy and terribly windy. 'Get closer,' he said over his shoulder, and I wriggled up behind him so that we were touching all the way down. I had my bag clutched under one arm and the other was tight round his waist. The leather jacket smelt wonderful. I was surprised at how solid and stable the bike felt. 'Where's this caff, then?' he asked. 'Left at the traffic lights,' I shouted in his ear. He leaned the bike over as we zoomed round the left-hand corner and I shut my eyes. 'Don't panic,' he said. After a few more corners I felt all right about it and we pulled up outside the back entrance to Mario's, where Liz worked. She was standing in the doorway, looking up the street, holding her bag. Then she saw it was me on the back of the bike and put her hands on her hips. 'Oh, bloody marvellous,' she said, sounding resigned.

I got off the bike and started to fiddle with the strap of my crash-helmet. Somehow I couldn't talk to Liz from inside the space capsule. 'You needn't bother,' said Liz. 'I can see you're going off with your greaser.' Nick pulled the bike on to its stand and came to help. He had taken his own helmet off and he undid the buckle on mine quickly. 'Look,' he said to Liz, 'I don't want to muck up your afternoon. I didn't know Sasha had arranged to go out with you until I turned up.' It was the first time I had heard him say my name.

'Matter of fact,' said Liz, 'we've got a pretty big party coming in tonight and there's a lot extra to do. I was just looking out to say I couldn't make it.'

Nick wasn't convinced. 'But you've got your bag with you,' he said. Liz didn't turn a hair. She said. 'Nipping down to Boots for some Tampax, aren't I?' There was nothing Nick could say to that. He looked at me and I said, 'Well if you're sure, Liz.' 'Course I'm sure, you twit,' she said. 'Go on – shove off and be careful.' She gave me a faint wink and said, 'I'll ring you later.'

'Okay,' I said. 'Thanks, Liz.'

'Nothing to thank *me* for,' she said, and set off down the street with her pale hair bouncing on her shoulders and her khaki canvas bag dangling in her hand.

'Great girl,' said Nick, looking after her.

'Yes, she is,' I said, happy that he liked her. 'She made it up, you know, about the big party tonight.'

'I know,' he said. 'Well, come on. Where shall we go?'

I had been thinking about it. I couldn't remember the names of any of the boring country villages we used to drive through when I was small but it came back to me that we used to stop for tea sometimes at a place called Westerham, and there was a stream that ran under a little wooden bridge between the car park and some ancient Cream Tea cottage the parents used to like.

'Westerham,' said Nick. 'Kent somewhere, innit?' He fished in the bike's top box and produced a dog-eared map. After a few minutes he said, 'Oh, I see. Through Bromley. No problem. Come on, then.' And we set off.

It was a marvellous afternoon. I remembered the little town from childhood and yet I was seeing it for the first time and it all seemed entirely different. With my parents, it had always been a solemn entry into the Cream Tea cottage, where we sat for ages under the black beams looking out of the diamond criss-crossed windows and I prayed that neither of them would choose the chocolate éclair from the plate of Mixed Fancies. And then we would saunter slowly down the village street looking in the dim windows of the antique shops where horse brasses hung on leather straps.

Today it was different. My legs felt a little shaky from being on the bike and the town seemed smaller and more open to the sky. We parked the bike outside a butcher's shop and walked past the green to where the church stood looking over the valley, and went in through the gate. Nick took my hand and we wandered along the steeply-sloping paths between the gravestones. The sun shone and it was very quiet and I thought that I must remember every detail of this day.

Nick said he got sick of London sometimes and I asked

him if he would like to live in the country. He wrinkled his nose and looked round warily at the yew trees and the distant hills and the misty sky where a glider climbed silently behind a little aeroplane and said, 'Dunno. There's a lot of world out there. I thought of joining the Merchant Navy.' A cold shadow seemed to fall across the afternoon. 'Oh, don't,' I begged him, and then regretted it, because he frowned and said, 'Why not?' I tried to sound light. 'Well,' I said, 'I've only just got to know you.' He stopped, and turned to face me. 'Look here, Lolly-top,' he said, 'don't start weaving spider's webs round me. I think you're terrific, and a really nice person, but I'm only twenty and I've got no job and I haven't done half the things I want to. I thought with all that crazy hair and the way you went for me in the shop, you were a girl who didn't give a damn. Someone who could be her own person.'

'I am,' I said quickly. 'It's the same for me. I want to go to art school and specialise in fashion and go to Paris and New York and –' I ran out of steam. It all hurt so much, and yet what I was saying was true. 'I mean,' I ploughed on, 'I've always thought women who give everything up to get married want their heads read, like I told you. Look at my parents. Talk about a fate worse than death!'

'That's all right, then,' he said. We walked on again. 'I had to get that clear,' he explained. 'Lots of girls have said I'm an absolute bastard for not getting involved – as if I'd let them down somehow. So I thought, next time I'll get it straight from the start, and if she doesn't like it then there's no harm done.'

'Right!' I said cheerfully. There was nothing else I could say, and a week ago I wouldn't have thought there was anything wrong with it. We set off up another path and the bulk of the church came between us and the sun. It was cool and dim and there were no flowers growing, just dark-leafed ivy. In a cramped corner beside the path where two walls met a tiny headstone stuck up out of the long grass. 'Must have been a small bloke they put in there,' Nick said. I bent and looked at the stone. I couldn't read the name but made out the mossy letters which said, 'Aged five days'. 'It's a baby,' I said.

We walked on a little way but the small tragedy tugged at my mind. Someone had wept for the baby but it lay there now in the damp ground, forgotten, grass-covered. And Nick would never love me. Suddenly I knew I was going to cry. I stared hard at a crisp bag which had been trodden on so often that it was flat and grey, but it was no good. A tear trickled down my cheek.

Nick stared at me incredulously. Then he put his arms round me. 'Hey,' he said gently, 'what is it?' I shook my head. 'Sorry,' I gulped, groping in my bag for a hanky. 'I always cry when I think about sad things.' I managed to smile at him, and blew my nose. Then he kissed me. In that moment all the coldness and feeling of isolation were swept away. Nick said, 'Aren't you lovely.' He sounded rather husky. We came round the side of the church into the sun and I was happy again, as if I had woken from a nightmare. 'Let's get out of this bloody churchyard,' he said. 'It's morbid.'

There was an ice-cream van standing on the green and Nick said, 'Come on, Lolly-top, I'll buy you a choc-ice.' We ran across to the van like kids and he bought two of those very expensive cone-things all wrapped in foil with coloured pictures. I wanted to pay for them but he shook his head firmly. 'What's the dole for?' he asked. We had a brief wrangle about him having paid for the petrol then I gave up. We sat down on the grass and ate our ices and I wished he would kiss me again. There was none of the irritated reluctance I had felt when I had been out with other boys. But Nick was not like other boys. Nick was not like anyone else. When I'd finished my ice cream I lay back on the grass and shut my eyes against the sun. Idly, I imagined living in some cottage in a place like this. Pots of home-made jam gleamed on the pantry shelf and I sat outside the back door in the evening sun, wearing a full-skirted blue dress with a white apron, shelling peas. And Nick came striding over the hill with a lamb across his shoulders.

'What we going to do this evening?' asked Nick. I sat up.

'I didn't tell Mum I'd be out,' I said. 'She'll be expecting me home for supper.' 'Ring her up,' said Nick simply. I looked at him, imagining what she would say if I rang up and told her I was in Westerham with a boy on a motor bike. But in the same moment I knew she would have to get used to it, and my dread slipped away. 'What shall we do, then?' I asked. 'You choose.' The ice cream had made me realise that I was hungry, for I hadn't brought any sandwiches today, being early closing day. I was worried about him not having much money. 'Get a Chinese take-away somewhere,' he said. 'Then go and have a drink. Play Space Invaders.'

'I'll go and ring Mum,' I said, getting up.

'Wait until we get back, it'll be cheaper,' he said practically. 'You don't want to ring from outside London. What's the time? About half-past four?'

I looked at my watch. 'Twenty past,' I said. He yawned and stretched. 'No need to go back yet,' he said. 'Let's go and find some better grass. This is all dogs and kids.'

We walked through the town until we came to a farm track and followed it past a barn and some open-sided buildings with tractors in them. We turned off the track onto a path which climbed steeply as it followed the rising ground. I looked back across the meadows to where a row of cottages stood on the far side of the road, and said, 'That's the place my parents used to go for tea.' He glanced at it and laughed. 'You needn't think *I'm* going there for tea,' he said. 'Three quid for scones and a dab of jam served by an old bag in a frilly apron? No, thanks.'

'Not on your life!' I agreed. There used to be minnows in the shaded water under the wooden bridge.

We climbed over a stile and came to a sloping meadow where the grass was long enough to shine silver in the sunlight. 'That's better,' Nick said happily. 'Now, that's proper country that is.' We climbed the slope, with our feet swishing through the long grass until there were no houses in sight. Nick sat down and said, 'Smashing.' I sat beside him and he put his arms round my shoulders. I turned my face towards him and we kissed. Then we were lying down. He slipped his hand inside my blouse and I felt his fingers creep over my breast. He touched my nipple and I stiffened all over because of the sudden shock that ran through me. 'You on the pill?' he whispered. For a moment, I almost told him I was. Then I said, 'No.' He took his hand away and ran it through my hair instead. 'You ever done it before?'

'No, I mean, I've had boy friends,' I said quickly, because I didn't want him to think I was just a kid, 'but there hasn't been much opportunity, living at home.'

'It's all right,' he said, looking away across the valley. He sat up with his arms round his knees, then turned his head and looked at me. 'Do you want to?' he asked.

I laughed breathlessly. 'You know I do,' I said. And it was true.

'You better get fixed up, then,' he said. I thought of Dr Jessup, and quailed. I had been to him two years ago when a cold had turned to sinusitis, and he had twinkled through his rimless glasses and said, 'My, my, aren't we getting a fine big girl.' He wore a waistcoat and his hands were fat. Oh, no, not Dr Jessup.

Nick pushed me gently down on the grass again and we kissed for a long time. Then he said, 'You don't want to worry about it. We can have a good time. Nobody goes on the pill unless they've got some reason to.'

'No,' I agreed.

He took his leather jacket off and put it on the grass under our heads. He was wearing a pin-tucked dress-shirt that day, with no collar, and unironed as always. I undid it down to the end of its opening and pushed it back, then rubbed my hand over his chest. He had only a few hairs between the firm muscles and his skin was brown and smooth. I loved the smell of him. I fingered the white shirt and said, 'Oxfam?' He laughed and said, 'How did you guess?' I said, 'You don't find cotton lawn like that in the shops. It's beautiful.'

'Be nice to have some money,' he said idly. 'I like clothes but I never buy any. Like other things better, I suppose.'

'I'll make you a shirt,' I promised him, and he gave me a lazy smile and said, 'Great.'

The sun began to dip down towards the top of the elm trees at the field's edge. I was ravenously hungry but I didn't want to cut this day short.

At last we got up to go, brushing bits of grass off each other. As we started to walk down the slope I looked back at the flattened patch in the grass where we had lain, and felt a kind of regret that the stalks and leaves would recover overnight so that tomorrow there would be no trace of us. Suddenly I understood why lovers carved their initials on trees. I could imagine, years later, running my fingers over the scarred letters and remembering the day we cut them.

It was cold on the bike going back to London despite the mildness of the evening, and my legs were blotched pink with the wind when we stopped by a phone box. My father answered and I felt guilty at once because I hadn't realised it was as late as that. 'Susan!' he said. 'Where are you? Your mother's worried sick.'

'She knew I was going out with Liz,' I said. She hadn't been listening last night for nothing.

'Yes, but she says you promised to do something to a dress for her,' said Dad. He sounded as if he was having a bad time. 'Are you coming home?'

'Well, no,' I said. 'That's what I've rung up to say. I've been asked out somewhere else, so I won't be in for supper. Tell Mum not to flap – I'll do her dress tomorrow night. She won't need it until the concert. She's just fussing.'

Dad gave his dry little laugh and said, 'You may be right.'

'Oh, I am,' I said confidently. 'Get stuck into one of your old books and take no notice.' We were always better on the phone than we were together, Dad and me. Perhaps it was because it didn't include Mum. He chuckled again and said, 'See you later, then, love. Thanks for ringing. 'Bye.' And he hung up.

Nick was sitting astride the bike outside the phone box. I gave him a thumbs-up sign. 'No bother,' I said. 'It was Dad, and he's all right.' Then I thought of Nick's father and said, 'Do you have to ring up or anything?'

'Nah,' said Nick. 'Left a note on the table. Said I'd gone to see about a job. He can't argue about that. At least,' he added as I climbed on the bike behind him, 'he can, but I don't have to take any notice.'

My frilly skirt really was a hopeless garment to ride a bike in. It blew up in the wind so much that my legs were bare all the way up and I was uncomfortably cold. But this time we weren't going far. The Chinese take-away was just down the end of the street.

When I went in through the back door Dad slipped into the kitchen. He cast a furtive glance over his shoulder and said, 'Trouble brewing, I'm afraid. Your friend Liz rang up and asked if you were in.'

'Oh, Lord,' I said, rubbing my arms to try and warm them. Dad gave a slight jerk of his head towards the road and said, 'Motor bike?' I nodded – and Mum came in. She folded her arms and leaned back against the door she had shut behind her. 'So,' she said. 'You're telling me lies. Why?'

'I didn't actually tell you anything,' I said. Dad went over to the sink and started to fill the kettle.

'You gave me to understand that you were out with Liz,' said Mum. 'And you weren't.'

'Look,' I said, 'I'm seventeen. I'm not your little girl any longer. I've got a life of my own to live. I don't have to run to you for permission every time I want to leave the house.'

'You'll always be my little girl,' she said. Tears welled in her eyes but she blinked them away angrily. 'I worry about you. I suppose you've been out with some boy, but you pick such awful boys. Look at that one you used to go to discos with – Roy something.'

'Blakely,' I said. 'Why pick him? There were plenty of others.' Somehow I wanted to shock her. She didn't have to know that Nick was the first boy who had ever meant anything to me.

'There is no need to make yourself out to be worse than you are,' she said.

'Oh, I don't know,' I said idly. 'It's rather fun. There's something so appealing about squalor.'

My father, standing beside the kettle, suddenly began to laugh. Mum glared at him. 'David!' she snapped. 'How typical of you to make it into a cheap joke! You have always undermined my authority, haven't you? Always managed to get Susan on your side so that the two of you can snigger behind my back. Well, all right. I wash my hands of it. And when some disaster happens you'll know whose fault it is, won't you?' She slammed out.

Dad raised his eyebrows and his shoulders and his hands in a huge shrug. He threw a couple of tea bags into the pot and filled it with boiling water from the kettle. 'I'll take her a cuppa,' he said, and fished the tray from its slot beside the dish-washer. When he had assembled the tea things he said, 'Do you want one?'

I shook my head. 'No, thanks,' I said. 'I'm full of beer.'

He laughed. 'Open the door for me,' he said, picking up the tray. I did as he asked. Just as I was going to shut the door behind him he looked over his shoulder and took a confidential step backwards. 'I used to have a Norton,' he said, 'before I knew your mother.' Then he went on into the sitting-room.

Chapter 6

I saw Nick at lunch-time on Thursday and Friday and was late back to the shop on both days. He came to collect me after work each evening and we went to Ron's café. The chap in there, Ron himself, soon got to know us and said, 'Hello. Two coffees, two biscuits?' I liked being known in Ron's café. It made me feel very warm and confident.

On Saturday it was much cooler and I turned up at the shop in jeans because Nick and I had arranged to go out after work and I wanted something practical to ride the bike in. Mrs Marshall was scandalised. 'That is *not* suitable dress for a shop assistant, Miss Bowman,' she said. 'You will go home during your lunch hour and change into something more acceptable.'

'Can't,' I said.

'And why not, may I ask?'

'Mum's out and she won't give me a key,' I said pathetically, hoping she wouldn't twig that it was a lie. She looked embarrassed. 'Oh.' She said crossly, 'Well, kindly come properly dressed on Monday.'

Mr Biggs had said his little piece when he gave me my pay packet on Friday. 'Er, Sasha, I wouldn't like to think you are getting into bad habits.'

'Bad habits, Mr Biggs?' I said innocently. Why should I make it easy for him?

'Yes,' he said. 'Coming in late from lunch. I can see that there are some – er – attractions to the lunch-break now, and I must say I find that a little surprising, all things considered.' He gazed at me reproachfully. 'I don't want to wield the big stick, Sasha,' he went on, 'but I'm afraid you must remember that there are plenty of other girls who would like your job. You will not be hard to replace.'

That brought me up short. 'I know,' I said seriously. 'I'm sorry, Mr Biggs. I'll try and watch the time.' I really didn't want to lose that job. He gave me a grim little smile and said 'Do that, Sasha.' So on Saturday I made sure to get back from the park on the dot, specially as I had already upset them through wearing jeans.

Nick came to the shop when we closed at half-past five. It still made me feel short of breath when I saw him. We went for a coffee at Ron's and Nick said he wanted to go to some place in Essex to see a chap who had a bike part he particularly wanted. Nick had bought a crashed Triumph some time ago, very cheaply, and he was rebuilding it in a friend's garage. 'Trouble with living in a flat is, you can't *do* anything,' he said. I hadn't thought about it before, but I saw what he meant.

The place in Essex turned out to be a huge café next door to a garage. The forecourt outside was crammed with bikes and their riders filled the café. Some of them had studs in their leather jackets and teeth painted on their helmets to give them a ferocious Japanese look, others had dirty faces and wore Barber suits, and the less well-off were in anoraks. The girls talked loudly, laughing and flicking ash on the floor. Most of them were in jeans and boots, with low-cut tops under their jackets. When I took my crash-helmet off and they saw my pink hair they seemed to think I was all right, and one or two of them asked where we came from and what sort of bike we had. 'Superdream,' I said as if I had been used to bikes for years. Nick found his friend and started a long, technical conversation about bike engines. One of the girls took her feet off the seat beside her and said to me 'Wanna sit down?' I slid into the place gratefully, glad to feel that I belonged.

Nick brought me some coffee and said, 'You all right? Sorry about the techno-babble. Won't be long.' I said I was fine. When he had gone one of the girls said, 'Isn't your boy friend smashing-looking!' I felt a great glow of pride but I just said, 'Hands off!' It was great pretending to be a tough biking girl. In fact, for a while at that time I thought I really was tough. Riding a motor bike made you feel like that. Bikes were like living things in a way, quick to understand your intentions. Nick said if I got a provisional licence he would teach me to drive and although the idea frightened me a bit, I was longing to try it. I envied the girls in the café who had their own bikes. They were somehow different from the pillion girls. Although the boys teased them you could see that they weren't worried.

We stayed in the café all evening, and had egg and chips, then drove home through Leytonstone and the closed-up City. 'Want to go round the West End?' Nick asked over his shoulder. 'Oh, yes, please!' I said. Being on the back of a bike was a great way to see London. I hadn't realised before how much the roof of a car restricts your vision. On a bike you can see all round you, and you can put your head back and look up at the tops of the buildings. Going round Trafalgar Square I saw the moon just above the figure of Nelson on top of his column, and thought, the same moon is shining on the field where we lay on Wednesday, where the grass was flattened.

At last we got back to my house and I climbed off the bike regretfully. I was getting very fond of it. 'See you tomorrow?' asked Nick. He switched the engine off and pulled the bike back onto its stand. 'I expect Liz will be coming round,' I said. 'She usually does on Sundays. Only in the morning, though.'

He thought, then asked, 'Does she have a boy friend?' I said she'd been going out with Gary, but I wasn't sure if he was an actual boy friend, and he said, 'Same as us.' Then he suggested we might go somewhere in the evening with Liz and Gary, and said he would pick me up at half-past seven anyway.

Out of the corner of my eye I could see the sitting-room curtain move, and knew that Mum was looking out. It made me feel uncomfortable and although I wanted Nick to kiss me, I didn't like the thought of standing there on the pavement with my mother watching us.

Nick put his arms round me and said, 'What's the matter? You've gone all stiff.' I explained about Mum and he put two fingers up at the window. 'Oh, Lord,' I said, half-horrified and half-laughing, 'I hope she didn't see that.'

'Serve her right if she did,' he said. 'I can't stand that sort of thing.' And without even looking back at me he got on the bike and rode off.

I went inside, and went straight up to my room. I wished I hadn't said anything about Mum watching. I wished Nick wanted to go somewhere just with me tomorrow. I wished he hadn't said, 'Same as us.'

I stood in the middle of the room, trying to be sensible. There was no need to be upset. He'd always made it clear that he didn't want to get involved. But as I stared round, all the familiar things I had known since childhood seemed pointless and silly. It was too late to be uninvolved. I wound up the gramophone and put on 'Goodbye, Summer' then lay on my bed and wept. I seemed to be saying goodbye to everything I used to be, and there was nothing to replace it except the hard business of learning to be tough and indifferent. I thought of my mother's sagging face and flabby arms, and my father's bitter patience, and was filled with dread. Was that what lay ahead for me? Lack of surprise, lack of resentment, lack of delight? As the long-dead voice sang on, I did not know whether I wept for the present pain or for the fear of its ending.

Mum banged on the door and shouted, 'Do you want a cup of tea?' I said, 'No, thanks,' but she banged again and shouted, 'Susan! Cup of tea?' I suppose the record was too loud for her to hear me. Anyway, it ended at that moment and I got up and took it off. I looked at the door and said, 'I'll be down in a minute.' At least she hadn't sounded cross. Perhaps she hadn't seen Nick's gesture. And I wanted even the little comfort which a cup of tea with my parents offered.

I washed my face before I went down, and put on some fresh mascara, but when I went into the sitting-room Mum and Dad both smiled at me so kindly that I could see they knew I'd been crying. They didn't mention Nick. Mum was still pleased because I'd done her dress for her on Thursday night. She asked me what sort of clothes she should get for the autumn and I thought blackly that she was humouring a lunatic. But it was better than having a row.

Liz did get her hair cut. When she came round that Sunday it was quite short, with wispy bits in front of the ears. She stood in front of the mirror, twiddling the wisps between a licked finger and thumb. 'I wish I could get them to be kiss curls,' she said. 'Like Liza Minelli had in "Cabaret", do you remember?'

Privately, I thought she did, as I had predicted, look rather like a camel, but I didn't say so. 'She's got silky black hair,' I said, 'and yours is ginger and wavy. You could get it straightened, of course.'

Liz turned away from the mirror. 'Quite honestly,' she said, 'I can't be bothered.' She flopped down on the bed, leaning back against the pillows. 'How are you, anyway?' she asked. 'I haven't seen you all week. How's this bloke?'

'He's great,' I said. Then I added, 'He's suggesting we might all go somewhere this evening. You and Gary and him and me.'

'That'd be nice,' Liz said, but she was still looking at me thoughtfully. '*Really* great?' she asked.

'Yes, really.' I went and looked out of the window. 'Liz,' I said, 'I do wish he cared.'

'Give him time,' said Liz. 'Men hate being hustled.' She frowned at me and added, 'What are you on about, anyway? I thought you were the great feminist, always saying how women threw their lives away for the sake of some bloke.'

'Yes, of course I am,' I said quickly. 'I still want to have a career and everything. I haven't changed.'

'Not much!' said Liz.

'I haven't!' I protested. 'I want to go to art school and be a designer and travel and everything, just the same. But that doesn't mean I can't have a relationship with anyone, does it?'

Liz was leafing through the drawings which littered my bedside table. 'Not much fashion about this lot,' she said, holding up a sheaf of them. They were my attempted sketches of Nick. 'They're just doodles,' I said crossly. I came and sat

62

on the other end of the bed and we looked at each other. 'Oh, Liz,' I said, 'it's such a funny summer. Things *are* changing. Not just me. Everything.'

She nodded. 'It's gone a bit weird,' she said. 'It's these blooming men. They get in the way. I mean, Gary's all right – he's fun and he's got a car and money and everything, and I like being with him, but I can see he's going to want to marry me or something. And I couldn't do that. I'd run a mile.'

I said, 'You should be so lucky,' and then regretted it. What was I saying? Liz thought it was peculiar, too. 'I don't understand you,' she said. 'Have a boy friend by all means. Have sex if you want to. But you don't have to commit your whole life to someone.'

'I know,' I said. 'That's exactly what I've always thought. But I feel as if he's part of me. Being without him would be like tearing off a leg or – or losing part of my brain. I think about him all the time, the things he says, the way his eyes crinkle at the corners when he smiles. The smell of him and the feel of him.'

Liz sighed. 'You *have* got it bad,' she said. 'I used to feel like that about Tony Green.'

I stared at her. Tony Green had been in the Sixth Form when we were in the fourth year, before I knew Liz very well. '*Did* you?' I said. 'But how did you get to know him?'

'I had a Saturday job in a cake shop,' she said. 'Told them I was sixteen and they believed it, like twits. He used to come in there with his mates for doughnuts. I think they had a thing about our doughnuts, they used to buy ever so many. Anyway, he asked me out and I went, and I thought the sun shone out of his bottom. I don't think I'll ever feel the same about anyone else.'

'Liz! You never told me,' I said. 'What happened?'

She shrugged. 'He went off to university,' she said. 'Never wrote or anything. Can't blame him, really.'

'Fancy you never saying,' I said.

Liz looked at me and said, 'Some things really hurt. You can't tell anyone unless you think they'll understand.'

I nodded slowly. Now, because of Nick, I understood.

'Won't you really feel the same?' I asked. 'Not about anyone?' She shook her head. 'Shouldn't think so,' she said. 'It wouldn't take me by surprise, you see.'

There it was again. Patience. Withdrawal. Self-protection. Had any of these people really felt the way I did? It seemed impossible. 'I know it's silly,' I said, 'but I just can't help it. If I think about controlling it or making it less, I feel as if I'm killing something. Killing me. I just can't bear it.'

Liz said, 'Now you know why women chuck everything up.'

'It can't be,' I said. 'I bet most of them are just bored and think it's an easy option, or they just fancy someone. The way I feel about Nick - it's not women's magazine stories.'

'I know,' said Liz. 'It's Romeo and Juliet.' She looked at me steadily, not joking, and added, 'But that's the way everyone feels.'

Everyone. Every single person. 'Oh, Liz,' I said, 'what am I going to do?'

'Sweat it out,' she said, 'like a fever.'

'I can't even wish it never started,' I said miserably.

'Well,' said Liz philosophically, 'as we've always said, it's all experience.' But this time our old rallying cry didn't work. I couldn't smile.

That evening Nick and I went round to Liz's house. It was part of a Victorian terrace round the corner from the Underground station, and Nick approved of it. 'Don't know why they had to knock all these old houses down,' he said. 'They're much better than flats. You can park a bike in the front and there's a bit of a garden at the back where you could have a shed. Repair things or keep a few rabbits. Dad used to keep rabbits before we moved to the flat.'

Gary's car was parked outside the house. I wouldn't have known it was his except that it had 'Gary' and 'Liz' in big white letters across the top of the windscreen. Indoors, Liz sat on Gary's lap in an armchair in front of the television. Liz's mother said, 'You lot want a cup of tea?'

'No, thanks,' said Liz, still looking at the screen. 'We're going out.'

'Well, shift yourselves, then,' said her mother, lighting a cigarette. She got an ironing-board out of the cupboard and set it up in front of the television set. 'Music while you work,' she said. 'Not that Sunday's much good on telly but it's better than nothing.' She up-ended the iron on the bit of tin at the end of the ironing-board and plugged it in. Liz got up. 'Better get out of here before we get draped with pillowcases,' she said. 'If you're not dashing about she thinks you're a clothes-horse.'

'Oh, go on out,' said her mother. 'Goodness sake. You clutter the place up.' Some ash fell from the cigarette in her mouth onto the ironing-board and she brushed at it vaguely then took a folded blouse off the top of the pile of clothes which lay in a blue plastic basket on the dining-table.

'Goodbye,' Mrs Lacey,' I said politely as we went out.

''Bye, love,' she said. Her eyes did not leave the television set.

Gary said, 'Might as well all go in the car.' He was a thin boy with short brown hair and sticking-out ears. It seemed funny to leave the bike behind and I had a pang of regret as Nick and I got into the back of the car and put our crash helmets on the shelf behind the back seat. When Gary started the engine, the car radio came on loudly and we moved off through the still-sunny streets in a gale of pop music. 'Where to?' shouted Gary over his shoulder.

'Richmond,' said Liz promptly. 'I want to go to that place by the river. It's good there.'

Nick was staring out of the window but he took my hand in his and began to explore it with his fingers, gently pressing my knuckles and touching the ends of my finger-tips. After a little while he said quietly, 'Have you got any money?' I nodded. The radio was so loud that I knew Liz and Gary couldn't hear what we said. 'I wasn't expecting to go anywhere expensive,' Nick said. 'If you could lend me a fiver –'

I got my purse out of my bag and gave him two five pound notes. He raised his eyebrows as if he was about to protest but I put my hand over his and said, 'It's all right.' He stuffed the notes into his jeans pocket then settled down with his arm round me and I stopped regretting the bike. I never minded where we were as long as I was with him. I didn't even worry about spending so much of the money I was supposed to be saving to go away with Liz. I still wanted to go, but I didn't like to think about it happening too soon. Leaving Nick would be dreadful, I pushed the thought away.

When we got to Richmond we went for a walk along the river and Nick and Gary started throwing stones into the water to try and make them skip. Nick caught at the overhanging branch of a tree and pulled himself up, then climbed higher into it. 'It's great up here!' he shouted down. Gary tried to climb up as well but he was wearing rather smart leather-soled shoes and he couldn't get a grip like Nick could in his old plimsolls. Nick sat in the tree making monkey noises and throwing down bits of twig and we stood about on the tow path waiting for him to come down.

Liz said, 'Is he always like this?' and I said, 'No, he's been rather well-behaved up to now, give or take a wind-up frog or two.' Suddenly I remembered the first time I had seen him, when he came into the shop and created such mayhem, and realised that he really had been amazingly polite since I had been going out with him. And so had I. In a way, Liz and I used to have more fun when we did things like going into shops and trying on all the wigs and putting on silly voices to suit the way we looked. We'd been thrown out of every shop that sold wigs for miles around. I wondered uneasily whether Nick was getting bored. But now, looking up at him gibbering in his tree, I began to feel angry. I was standing there in high heels and a white cotton dress all gathers and flounces, with beads in my hair, feeling stupid.

'Nick!' I shouted up at him, 'Come down! It's boring.' Liz and Gary were standing at the water's edge with their arms round each other's waists, looking at the bits and pieces that floated by in the river. 'Nick!' I said again. '*Please* come down!'

'Pick me up on your way back,' Nick said from his tree. 'I

like it up here.' And he scratched his armpit elaborately.

Suddenly I was blazing with rage. I stooped and grabbed up a stone and hurled it at him – and clapped my hands to my mouth in horror. The stone had hit him on the side of the forehead. He scrambled down from his perch and dropped to the ground. Blood was running down his face. 'Thanks a lot,' he said coldly.

'Oh, Nick, I didn't mean to,' I said in a panic, 'please don't be cross.'

He rubbed his face, then looked at the blood on his hand. Liz and Gary had come back from the river when he jumped down but neither of them had seen me throw the stone.

'Oh, Nick, what a mess,' said Liz practically. 'Can't take you anywhere!'

Nick glared at her. 'I'm not asking you to,' he said.

Liz was fishing some Kleenex out of her bag. Nick hauled the two five pound notes I had given him out of his pocket and slapped them into my hand. 'Keep your money,' he said. And he set off along the tow-path the way we had come, making no attempt to wipe the blood off his face.

'Stay there,' Gary said to Liz and me, and went after Nick.

'Take this!' called Liz, holding out the Kleenex. He came back for it then ran to catch Nick up. I didn't want to watch. I felt rather sick.

'What happened?' Liz asked me. When I told her, she said, 'Serve him right. You stick up for yourself, love. Don't start being a doormat. It's not your style.'

'So it seems,' I said weakly. 'What an awful thing to do!' But then I started to laugh.

'What was all that about the money?' Liz asked. I explained that Nick had said he wasn't expecting to go anywhere expensive and Liz thumped her forehead with her fist. 'Am I an idiot!' she exclaimed. 'Poor bloke! He must have been in a panic when I said I wanted to go to the place by the river. I bet he thought I meant that rather posh club. It costs a bomb in there. I was only talking about the pub that overlooks the water.'

'I don't know what he thought,' I said.

She looked at me and nodded. 'That's what it is. He thought he was being rushed into an expensive evening he wasn't dressed for and couldn't afford. No wonder he went and hid up a tree. What a nut case, though! Why didn't he just say?'

'Would you?' I retorted. 'When you've just met people for the first time and you're going out for the evening, would you really start a grovel about how you hadn't got a job and didn't have any money?'

'No,' Liz admitted. There was a pause. Nick and Gary had disappeared from sight. 'You'd lent him some money, though,' she said. 'He didn't have to be so beastly.' I nodded miserably. That's what I was thinking.

We waited there for quite a long time. At last Nick and Gary came back, walking side by side along the path. Nick's face was clean and he had a bit of sticking plaster over the cut on his forehead. He put out his hand and ruffled my hair. 'Sorry,' he said. But he didn't smile. I took his hand and said, 'So am I. Honestly, I never thought it would hit you. It was only like trying to scare a bird out of a tree.'

'That's why women are so lousy at cricket,' said Gary cheerfully. Liz said, 'Rubbish. We've got better things to do, that's all. Where did you get the Band-Aid?'

'He's got them in his car,' said Nick, nodding at Gary. 'Proper little Boy Scout. And I had a wash in the Gents under the bridge.'

'Right,' said Liz briskly, 'let's go and have a drink.'

Somehow it was Liz and I who set off together and the boys followed slowly behind us. They seemed to have taken a liking to each other, because when we looked back they were deep in conversation and I was glad about that. All the same, I couldn't get over the feeling that Nick would never forgive me, and I said so to Liz. 'Well, honestly, Sash, if he's like that you're better off without him,' she declared. 'I know he's the love of your life, but you'll survive.'

I thought, well, she should know. But I still couldn't bear to think about it.

The rest of the evening wasn't too bad, except Nick and

Gary spent the whole time talking about engines. I had forgotten that Gary worked in a garage and I hadn't at that time quite realised how fanatically enthusiastic Nick was about motor bike engines. Liz and I got pretty bored and I was quite glad when it was closing time. I hadn't had a chance to give back the money Nick had thrust at me so angrily, so I was surprised that he bought a round of drinks when it was his turn.

In the car, I sat in the corner of the back seat as far as I could get from Nick because I was sure he hadn't forgiven me. The radio was blaring and Gary and Liz were singing.

'Don't be like that,' said Nick, pulling me towards him. 'I said I was sorry, didn't I? What do I have to do?' He crouched in the well of the car and started to kiss my feet. 'Pardon, Your Majesty, oh, pardon, pardon!' he said passionately. 'Do not chop your humble servant's head off!'

I began to giggle and Liz looked round and said, 'What are you two doing? Hey – where's Nick? He hasn't fallen out, has he?'

'I shall if she doesn't forgive me,' said Nick dramatically. He opened the door and leaned out as Gary was going round a corner and I grabbed him by the top of his jeans.

'Pack it in!' shouted Gary.

Nick shut the door and got back onto the seat beside me. 'Got some good news,' he said.

'What?' I wasn't sure if he meant it.

'Gary's boss is looking for another mechanic. I'm going round there tomorrow, see if he'll take me on. Gary says he'll put in a word, so I might be able to swing it.'

'Oh, Nick, that's great!' I said. Then I added, stupidly, 'But I won't see you at lunch-times.'

'Don't be so daft,' Nick said. 'Even mechanics have got to eat. If our lunch-breaks are at the same time I'll still come and meet you.'

'Oh, *good*,' I said.

There was a pause. He was looking at me in an odd sort of way and then he said, 'Do you really love me, Lolly-top?'

'Oh, yes,' I said recklessly. 'I do.'

The lights from shop windows flashed across his face as we passed them. I looked away, feeling sure he would tell me not to be so silly. Not to get involved. But he said, 'I'm pretty fond of you, too.'

He had never said anything like that before. It was a moment of pure happiness.

Chapter 7

Nick didn't wait until lunch-time the next day. He came striding into the shop at twenty-eight minutes past eleven – I had been watching the clock, as usual – and said, 'I got it!' He was wearing a pair of black leather motor cycle boots with red piping round the tops and straps round the back of the ankles which he had left undone so that the buckles clinked as he walked.

'The job? Oh, great!' I said. 'When do you start?'

'Tomorrow morning. How d'you like my boots? Bought them from a bloke at the garage. He'll wait till Friday for the money. Only a tenner.'

'Do you want it now?' I asked eagerly. 'I'll lend it to you if you like, then you won't have to keep him waiting.'

'That'd be terrific,' he said apologetically, 'if you could. Gary lent me some last night but – '

Mrs Marshall came into the little kitchen while I was taking the money out of my purse and she looked at the notes in my hand. I must admit, she didn't actually refer to them. 'Miss Bowman,' she said, 'I have told you before, I will not have you bringing your friends to the shop. We have certain standards to keep up and young men such as the one out there are not desirable. Any customer might well think twice about coming into the shop.'

'Oh, stuff your shop,' I said cheerfully. She turned on her heel and walked out. I put my bag back in the locker then went out to give Nick the money. He looked absolutely marvellous in those boots. I kissed him and said, 'See you in the park.'

'Twelve-thirty,' he promised. 'Oh – can you get your lunch-break shifted? Mine's from one to two.'

'I'll try,' I said. And he went out.

71

Mrs Marshall had been behind the basketball boots, listening. She gave me a cod-eyed stare and said, 'There is no question of changing your lunch-break, Miss Bowman. And I am not satisfied with the state of those chair-seats. Go and wipe them again.'

I felt so happy that I suddenly thought of myself as a pantomime fairy and said, 'I fly to obey your command!' I blew her a kiss and flitted off to the kitchen on tip-toe, waving my arms. Mr Biggs covered his eyes with his hand.

We went down the market that evening and I bought a length of fabric to make Nick a shirt. It was dark maroon poplin. I had designed the shirt on a scrap of paper in Ron's, leaning on the plastic shelf between our empty coffee cups. Granddad neck opening, deep-set sleeves with turned-back cuffs and a flamboyant collar like I'd seen on a portrait of Oliver Cromwell. I went home all eagerness to get it started.

Dad was out again that night, and Mum sat watching the television but keeping half an eye on what I was doing as I cut out the fabric on the big table in the sitting-room. I used a blouse pattern as a rough guide, but allowed heaps more on the shoulders and arm length. The collar and neckband were tricky. I drew several versions on newspaper and cut them out, then draped them round my neck and inspected them in the mirror.

'I don't know how you can do that,' Mum said. 'I wouldn't dare.'

'It's perfectly safe,' I said. 'Once you know what the flat shapes look like when they're round a body you're all right.'

She put her head on one side as she inspected the collar I was trying on. 'It looks a bit big,' she said.

'Oh, it's not for me,' I told her casually. 'It's for Nick.'

She didn't seem horrified. 'Well,' she said thoughtfully, 'if you're actually making shirts for him ... Is he nice, this Nick?'

'He's very nice,' I said, marking out the collar I had decided on with tailor's chalk. 'His name's really Dominic.'

'What a pity he doesn't use it,' Mum said. 'So much more distinguished. And people always assume that Nick is short

72

for Nicholas.'

When she wasn't upset, Mum was all right to talk to, but I was always just a little bit careful. It was so easy to put a foot wrong and trigger off an outburst. 'Where's Dad this evening?' I asked.

'Taking a customer out to dinner,' she said. 'It's a good thing the Bank pays his expenses. The amount of entertaining he has to do, it would cost a packet.'

'Why do these people have to be taken out?' I asked. 'Can't they just do their business during banking hours, like everyone else?'

'Your father's very conscientious,' Mum said proudly. 'A lot of managers don't bother to take an interest in a customer's business but David says there's nothing like seeing for yourself. He had to go all round a chicken factory the other day. He said it was horrible.'

'I know,' I said. 'He was telling us over supper the other evening, wasn't he? That night you'd done chicken casserole. I could hardly eat it.'

'So he was,' she said. Then she sighed. 'I never remember if you're in or out these days.' Dangerous ground, I thought. Shifting away from it, I said, 'Well, at least you know he gets properly fed when he's out in the evening. You don't have to sit up with sandwiches or keep things hot.'

She sighed again. '*I* wouldn't mind being taken out to a meal occasionally,' she said. 'But he thinks it's a bore now. "You get sick of all this restaurant food", he says. But it makes him appreciate his home cooking.'

'Where does he take his customers?' I asked. 'Somewhere really posh?'

'Oh, I don't think so,' Mum said. 'I doubt if the Bank would run to the Ritz. No, he says you still can't beat Soho for decent food at a moderate price. He was saying the other day he's found quite a nice place in Frith Street. Italian. Up a flight of dark stairs beside a betting shop, he said it was. Nothing fancy. You know how he hates things like coloured lights.'

'Oh, yes,' I said. 'When I was little and we used to go out,

I always wanted to go into cafés that had orange lights low over the tables, and red vinyl seats – but no, it had to be somewhere dark and thatched.' I cut round the last of my pattern pieces and stacked them up carefully, then started picking up the waste bits off the floor. I always dropped the trimmings on the floor so I couldn't get mixed as to which bits I wanted and which I didn't, and Mum had stopped complaining about the mess after I pointed out that I had once cut a blouse yoke out of an already-cut sleeve.

Mum had been amazingly reasonable about Nick, I thought. And it was really very companionable to spend an evening with her like this, chatting in a relaxed sort of way. 'Nick and I went down to Westerham last week,' I said. 'It was funny to see it again after so long. It looked much smaller, somehow.'

Mum's face tightened and I knew I had made a mistake. 'I suppose I must get used to sitting at home,' she said bleakly.

'Well, you can't get three on a motor bike,' I pointed out, but she didn't smile. I gathered up my fabric pieces and made for the door. I had discovered from long experience that it was best to do my sewing upstairs.

Nick came stumping across the park at ten past one the next day wearing a navy blue boiler suit. 'You might have said you'd come straight here,' he grumbled. 'I've wasted all this time calling round at the shop for you.'

As usual, I was the one who felt guilty. I had been so interested in getting the fabric for his shirt yesterday that I'd forgotten to tell him I couldn't get my lunch-break changed. I explained and apologised and said, 'Have a sandwich.'

'Ta,' he said, taking one. He had washed his hands but there was black grease all round his finger nails. 'It's great to be working,' he said with his mouth full. 'I hate hanging about with nothing to do all day.'

I nodded. I knew exactly what he meant. 'What have you been doing?' I asked, and he said, 'Stripping a Transit engine.'

When we had finished the sandwiches and drunk the tins of Coke he got out his tobacco tin and rolled himself a cigarette. He lit it and leaned back on the bench, looking up at the tree above us and blowing a long cloud of smoke. 'Great out here,' he said. 'Makes you appreciate it when you're shut in a workshop all day.' After a few minutes he got up and pulled me to my feet. 'Let's go and find some grass,' he said.

We walked along the gravel path that led round the pond until we came to the wild part where bluebells grew in the spring. 'That's better,' he said as we swished through the coarse, dark green grass. He sat down amid a clump of young silver birch trees and I sat down beside him. 'The smell of engine oil always makes me feel randy,' he said. He undid my blouse and pushed his hand inside, and the electricity of excitement ran through me at once. The way he kissed me was hard and violent and I felt rather frightened at first, except that the excitement overcame it. 'Oh, Nick, I do love you,' I said.

He stared down at me through the dark lashes. 'We could go to my place,' he suggested. 'Not far on the bike. We'd have half an hour.'

'I can't,' I said. 'I've got to be back at half-past one.'

'Thought you loved me,' he murmured. He kissed my mouth and my neck and slipped my bra strap off my shoulder. 'Someone will see,' I said, but I didn't want him to think I was being prudish.

'So what?' he said. 'They'll just go home and give their wives a good time.'

'Or their husbands,' I said. I felt reckless. I wanted to go on and find out what it was all about. It was maddening to be so near and not to be able to go all the way. Nick must have felt the same, because after a while he rolled away from me and lay on his back with an arm across his face. I did up my blouse and wondered why I had chosen today to wear a bright pink lipstick. There couldn't be much of it left. Then I looked at my watch.

'Oh, Lord!' I said. 'It's gone ten to two!'

'Off you go, then,' he said, not moving.

I stood up, brushing my skirt and tucking in my blouse. 'See you this evening?' I asked. He took his arm away from his face and said, 'I don't get off until six. Wait for me in Ron's if you like.'

I said, 'All right.' Then I knelt down beside him and gave him a last kiss.

'Oh, why don't you get out of here?' he said angrily, and I got up and ran away from him across the grass until I caught my foot on an empty lemonade bottle and almost tripped. I slowed to a walk, panting for breath. Why was he so unkind? It wasn't my fault I only had half-an-hour with him. I ought to have done something about getting on the pill but there hadn't been time. And I shrank from telling some stranger what I intended to do when I couldn't quite imagine it even in my own mind. I wondered how Liz felt about Gary. She hadn't gone all the way with anyone yet, either, but she had always said that she would one of these days, when she found the right person. Someone special enough.

Mrs Marshall was standing in the shop doorway looking down the street as I approached. When she saw me she went inside and as I got to the door Mr Biggs was waiting for me.

'I must warn you, Sasha,' he said, 'that this is the last chance I shall give you. It's past two o'clock and you are more than half-an-hour late. What's more, I understand that you were extremely rude to Mrs Marshall yesterday. You will apologise to her and it is not to occur again, do you understand?'

'Yes,' I panted. I had run almost all the way back from the park.

'You had better go and tidy yourself up,' he said severely.

When I got to the little kitchen and looked at myself in the cracked mirror over the sink I saw what he meant. There was a long piece of grass in my hair and my lipstick was smudged all over my mouth. What's more, there were grass stains on both sleeves of my white blouse and grey finger marks round the buttons. I looked at my battered reflection with sympathy and reproach. Oh, dear, I said to it silently, just look what the cat brought in.

Mrs Marshall came through the door and stood behind me. I wished she had waited until I looked a bit better. I turned to face her and said, 'I'm sorry I was rude to you, Mrs Marshall. I didn't mean to be.'

For a moment she said nothing, and when she did speak it was in a different tone from her usual sarcasm. 'I'm sorry, too,' she said. She had obviously decided to make an effort with me. 'It makes me *very* sorry to see a youngster messing up her life. I must admit,' she went on before I could say anything, 'when you first came here I thought you were a silly girl, with your hair and everything, but Mr Biggs insisted on giving you a chance and I respect his judgement. You learned the work quickly and I thought you had promise.'

Promise, I thought wildly. As a shop assistant? That wasn't a promise, it was a threat. But Mrs Marshall hadn't finished. She took a step nearer and put her plump hand on my arm. 'Don't throw yourself at the first boy you meet, my dear,' she said. 'Believe me, he's not unique, however it may seem. There are plenty more of them about.'

I froze. How dare she talk about Nick like that? She didn't know anything about him. 'Thank you, Mrs Marshall,' I said coldly. 'I'll bear your views in mind.' I turned my back on her and started to comb my hair. It wasn't so curly now because rags were such a fiddly business that I'd been using rollers instead. I thought gloomily that it looked a bit like tinned spaghetti. Through the mirror I saw Mrs Marshall watching me, but after a few moments she went back to the shop.

Liz came in that afternoon and I glanced round, expecting an explosion from Mrs Marshall, but saw with relief that she had gone into the stock cupboard with Mr Biggs, probably to check the new autumn shoes which had arrived in the morning.

'Oh, Liz,' I said, 'I'm so glad to see you.'

'What's the matter, love?' she asked. I told her all about being late back from the park and what had happened with Nick and how it looked as if I was going to lose my job. 'And, Liz,' I ended, 'I've *got* to do something about going on the

77

pill and I just can't face Dr Jessup.'

She perched on the Offer Bin and said, 'What d'you mean, you've got to?'

'Well, I want to,' I amended. 'I mean, I think that's why he went so funny in the park because, if he's had girl friends who go all the way and I don't . . .' My voice tailed off. Then I asked, 'What are you going to do about Gary?'

'He can blooming well wait,' said Liz. 'When I really want to I will, but I'm not going to muck up all my hormones by going on the pill for the first bloke who wants to get my pants down.'

'But don't you want to?' I asked curiously. 'I do. It's driving me insane.'

'I felt like that about Tony,' said Liz. 'But of course I never got the chance.' She frowned. 'I don't know. Sex and love aren't quite the same thing. I always thought they had to go together but I'm not so sure now. You can waste an awful lot of time waiting for someone really special. I mean, you've got to live, haven't you?'

'But Nick *is* special,' I said obstinately. 'And he's going to get fed up with just lying on the grass and all that. He wanted me to go to the flat with him today.'

'You want your head read,' said Liz. '*Any* bloke will say that. If he really cared about you as a person he wouldn't be trying to haul you into bed regardless of how you feel.'

'I seem to be in such a muddle about it,' I said unhappily. 'When I'm with him I get so worked up, I can't think about anything else. It seems to be all that matters. In between times, like now, I think of it in a different sort of way and the idea sort of scares me. Silly, isn't it?'

'I don't think it's a bit silly,' said Liz. 'It's your body and nobody can make you do anything with it unless you want to. Otherwise, like you said, it's just a sell-out. But if you really want to get fixed up, Maureen says the place to go is the Family Planning Clinic, round the back of the hospital. She says they're really nice in there.' Liz glanced past me and got off the Offer Bin. I looked round and saw that Mrs Marshall had come out of the stock cupboard and was looking at us pointedly, although she hadn't come over. 'Better go,' said Liz. 'Listen, I've got a day off on Thursday. What about doing something in the evening?'

'Meet me here at half-past five,' I said, tidying the desert boots energetically. 'Right,' said Liz, and went out. On Thursday, I thought, I wouldn't be waiting for Nick in Ron's, and serve him right for being so bad-tempered. I gave Mrs Marshall a tentative smile and she smiled encouragingly back. It made her look almost attractive.

Since I had promised to meet Nick at Ron's that evening I went along there after work. I was afraid he would still be in a bad mood but I couldn't stay away. I pushed open the glass door and Ron looked up from behind the steaming tea urn and said, 'Two coffees, two biscuits?'

'He isn't here yet,' I said. 'Got himself a job.'

'Glad to hear it,' said Ron. The place was emptier than usual and I slid into one of the seats beside a table. I had bought a magazine to read while I was waiting because I still hated the feeling of hanging around on my own. Ron brought me a cup of his funny-tasting coffee and a biscuit, and nodded at the magazine. 'Lot of money, aren't they,' he said, 'for what they are. Nearly all adverts.'

I thought it was nice of him to talk to me. 'I can't resist them,' I said. 'I always think they're going to be fabulous, but they never are.'

'That's life, innit,' said Ron. He wiped his hands on the teacloth he wore tucked into the waist of his trousers as an apron and added, 'Who's taken old Nick on, then?'

'Bennett's Garage,' I told him. 'He's rebuilding engines.'

Ron nodded. He had a long, meaty face with a broken nose that went sideways. 'Let's hope he keeps it, then,' he said. He brushed a few crumbs off the table with his hand then added, 'You want to watch Nick, you know.' I felt my face turn scarlet. I looked down at my coffee and stirred it busily although I didn't take sugar. 'Hope you won't mind me saying,' Ron went on, 'but he's got a bit of a reputation, has Nick.' I still didn't say anything. 'I've always said he's a good

79

lad at heart,' said Ron. 'I've covered up for him many a time when some girl's come in here looking for him and I've known he was out with a different one. But I reckon someone like you who knows what she's about can manage him fine. You want to know the score before you start, that's all. Then you don't get any nasty surprises, do you?' He laughed, looking me up and down and giving me a knowing wink and a shake of the hand. 'Like I say, I reckon you can manage him.'

'I reckon so,' I said bravely and Ron, with another wink, went back behind his counter.

I turned the pages of the magazine nonchalantly but I couldn't read anything and my eyes hopped from picture to picture. I wished I was as bold as my pink hair made me look.

It seemed a long time before Nick came striding in with the buckles clinking on his boots, and slumped into the seat opposite me. 'What a day!' he said. 'I'm knackered.' He leaned across the table and kissed me then shouted, 'Two coffees, two biscuits, Ron!'

Ron, washing cups in the sink under the counter, took no notice.

'Say please,' I told Nick. He seemed quite unconcerned about the events of our lunch hour.

'He knows what I mean,' he said. Then he smiled at me and added, 'Thanks for coming. I didn't know if you'd be here.' So perhaps he was concerned about it after all.

'I'll always be here,' I said, and I meant it. Nick didn't answer. He seemed to be thinking about something else. 'There's some overtime work with this job,' he said. 'If I want it, that is. Thought it wouldn't be a bad idea. Pick up some cash.'

'What will it mean?' I asked.

'I can do a couple of hours a night,' he said. 'Knock off at eight instead of six.' I tried not to look disappointed but I couldn't have succeeded very well, because he put his hand over mine and said, 'Tell you what we'll do. Friday night, when I get paid, we'll go up West and have a slap-up meal somewhere. All right? Make up for not coming in here.'

'It's hardly worth it if you don't get off till eight,' I said.

80

And suddenly I could hear my mother's voice saying those words, peevish and complaining. Nick frowned impatiently. 'I'll knock off at six that night, stupid,' he said. 'Got to have a bath and change, haven't I?'

I put my hand over his and squeezed it. 'Yes, of course,' I said. 'It'll be super. Really great.'

'Where shall we go?' he asked. 'D'you know anywhere good? Not the bloody Ritz,' he added.

I thought of my conversation with Mum last night and said, 'There's quite a decent little place in Frith Street.' I didn't mind him thinking I'd been there myself. 'It's up a flight of stairs beside a betting shop,' I added. He looked at me and grinned. 'You know your way around a bit, then,' he said.

Ron brought two coffees and two biscuits and said to Nick, 'You paying today?' Nick shook his head cheerfully. 'Got no money till Friday,' he said. 'You'll have to ask the missus.'

'Bloody marvellous,' said Ron. He looked at me and added, 'Don't know how you put up with him, love.'

'Nor do I,' I said. But I was feeling so warm because of Nick's description of me as 'the missus' that I ignored Ron's wink as he went back to the counter. Ron could keep his opinions to himself.

Chapter 8

The next day was Wednesday, Early Closing Day again. This time last week we had gone on the magical trip to Westerham. I brought sandwiches and went to the park as usual so that at least we could meet for lunch. I didn't want to start eating our picnic until he arrived but at twenty-past-two I opened the packet of sandwiches and ate one slowly, still expecting at any minute to see him come running across the grass.

I waited until three o'clock then walked home. Even then, I half expected him to come up beside me on the bike, full of apologies and explanations. Why should it matter so much? I got on with making his shirt. At least the fabric was something we had chosen together. It wasn't much of a link, but it was better than nothing.

On Thursday I went to the park again, and waited. It seemed like something out of a dream when he did at last come across the grass, not running but wandering along inattentively as he rolled himself a cigarette. He licked it and stuck it down as he reached me and flopped down on the bench. 'Hello,' he said, striking a match. He lit his cigarette and flicked the still-burning match away. I said rather crossly, 'Where have you been?'

'Working,' he said as though stating the obvious. 'Not like shop work, you know. If you get really stuck into a job you can't just drop it and run off when the clock strikes one.'

I said, 'Well, have a sandwich quickly. I'll have to go in five minutes.'

'You don't have to worry,' he said. 'There's no panic for money now I'm working. Tell them to stick their job. You could work part-time or something. Then there wouldn't be this fuss about lunchtimes.'

I stared at him. I couldn't forget what Liz had said. 'If you really cared about me as a person,' I said recklessly, 'you wouldn't expect me to give up my job just so that I could be there at your convenience.'

He took my hand and said, 'If I didn't care, I wouldn't want you, would I?'

My stomach churned with the excitement which always made it so difficult to remember what I really thought. I tried to keep hold of my common sense. 'I've got to have some money,' I insisted. 'I told you, Liz and I want to go on holiday. We planned it before I even met you.'

He trod the cigarette out and took a sandwich. 'All right for some,' he said. 'No use me hoping for a holiday, is it?'

'That's not *my* fault,' I said. I pushed the whole bag of sandwiches at him, and the two tins of Coke, and added, 'I've got to go.'

He shrugged. 'If you want to. See you in Ron's, then.'

'No, you won't, actually,' I told him. 'I'm going out with Liz tonight.' And I ran off across the grass, trying not to wish I was going to Ron's instead.

Liz and I decided not to spend any money that evening because it would take up too much of our holiday fund. I began to feel excited about it again, for while I was with Liz it really did seem as if we were certain to go on our trip. We walked up and down the High Street talking about our holiday and looking in shop windows in case there were any interesting clothes. I was always in search of new ideas. Then we went back to Liz's house. Her mother was sitting in front of the television set with a cigarette in one hand and an ashtray in the other. We had a cup of tea with her then went up to Liz's little room that overlooked the street.

Inevitably, we talked about Nick and Gary. We agreed that there was no reason why anyone shouldn't have a close relationship with someone else and still pursue a career and keep a proper sense of self-respect. Nick, I decided, would have to understand that I had my rights, too, the same as he did. Or else.

It was easy to be sensible when Liz was sitting there on the

83

other end of the bed. Although she was wearing an ancient spangly cocktail dress, her short hair made her look business-like and we both felt that we were being no more than completely reasonable. But I knew it would be different when I was with Nick. The awful thing was, a part of me didn't even *want* to be reasonable.

Nick came to our bench in the park in good time the next day. He was in a nice mood and the sun was hot, shining down through the yellowing leaves to make dappled patches on the ground. I wished we were in the proper country where the air smelt fresh and there were no bottles and cans and sweet wrappers lying about on the grass. 'All set for tonight?' he asked. I smiled at him and nodded without answering because my cheeks were bulging with the apple I was eating. I had dreamed last night about going out to a meal in a restaurant with Nick but I didn't want to think about it. In my dream Nick had gone to talk to a man about a motor bike and they had walked out of the door together, and a bullying waiter was shouting at me because I could not pay the bill.

'I'll pick you up at half-past seven,' he said. I promised to be ready.

Nick dug about in the sandwich packet as hungrily as a dog in a dustbin, and inspected the one he selected. 'Cor, beef,' he said. 'Your Mum makes smashing sarnies.'

'Actually,' I said with dignity, 'I make my own sarnies.'

'Who's a clever girl, then,' he said with his mouth full. And I knew he didn't care who made the sandwiches as long as they were there. I didn't mind, though. We were both happy and when we had finished eating he put his arm round me and we sat there contentedly in the warm sun.

I was ten minutes late back at the shop but I didn't think it mattered because I had stayed on at least as long as that after half-past twelve. There had been a lot of shoes to clear up after a fussy woman, who wanted something special for her ruby wedding but had one foot bigger than the other. She hadn't bought anything, but that wasn't my fault. As Nick observed when I told him about her, she wanted a blacksmith's, not a shoe shop. And Mr Biggs had paid me for my week's work this morning, and made no mention of replacing me with someone else. Things seemed to be going well.

I couldn't decide what to wear that evening. There was no point in wearing a pretty dress that would get horribly crushed or blow about all over the place on the bike, and I wanted to make sure I was warm enough. When I got cold my nose always ran and I looked a real mess. I had made a pair of matador pants out of black cotton printed with a gold pattern and I decided on those over black tights, with a ruffled white shirt and a quilted waistcoat.

I had bought three packets of pipe cleaners from a tobacco shop on the way home. I used these to twist my hair into ringlets when I had washed it and refreshed the pink dye. They worked beautifully. I was just doing my make-up when Nick rang the bell and I heard Mum open the door. When I got down to the sitting-room he was settled in an armchair with a glass of sherry in his hand while Mum, between sips of her own sherry, told him how she had nearly married a fellow-student at the Royal College of Music who had since become a famous conductor. I had heard the story many times before. 'We went to a fair,' she was telling Nick, 'and Carlo insisted on going into the fortune teller's tent and having our palms read. Gypsy Rose Lee or something I don't suppose she was a real gypsy, just an old woman with gold ear-rings and a red duster tied round her head, but I'll always remember what she said. "Your destiny is in your own hands, my dear. There may be great happiness in store for you, but you must beware of a rash move. A wrong decision may spoil everything."'

'And did it?' asked Nick.

'I've never been sure,' Mum said. 'A few weeks later Carlo asked me to go to Italy with him because a friend of the family had offered him the chance to conduct at a festival somewhere. But it would have meant I missed my final exams. It was all right for Carlo, he was a post-graduate student – but I thought it was the rash move the gypsy meant.'

'So you didn't go?' asked Nick.

'No,' said Mum. She sighed. 'Carlo met a girl in Italy and married her. And I passed my exams and got a teaching job and then got married and had Susan.'

'Susan?' enquired Nick.

Mum frowned slightly. 'Oh – Sasha, then. I keep forgetting.' Nick looked at me and raised his eyebrows but Mum was going on, 'I think I was wrong. The rash move was staying at College. Otherwise I wouldn't have ended up like this, would I, stuck alone in a house while everyone is out enjoying themselves.'

I wished Dad had been in that evening. It always seemed much worse to say goodbye to Mum when he wasn't there.

Nick finished his sherry and said, 'Sounds as if the old bird in a red duster was hedging her bets, if you ask me. Heads you lose, tails I win. I mean, nobody's life ever goes dead right all the way, does it?'

Mum sighed. 'So I have discovered,' she said.

Nick stood up and said, 'Time we were off. Thanks for the drink, Mrs Bowman. See you later.' And to my great relief, he marched me out before she could say any more, even though he did say, 'Come along, Susan!' I glared at him.

'Getting a bit heavy, wasn't it?' he said as we stood beside the bike putting on our crash helmets.

I said, 'Well, I told you what she's like. Convinced she's missed out somewhere. The trouble is, it has to be somebody's fault.'

'No wonder your dad stays out,' said Nick.

Luckily I spotted the doorway of the restaurant as we rode past. I pointed it out to Nick and we parked the bike in Soho Square and walked back through the narrow streets, which seemed to be full of people talking or arguing or trying to sell things – mostly sex, in one form or another. The restaurant was plainly furnished with ordinary wooden chairs and tables, and I could see why Dad liked it. Although the tablecloths were of stiff, much-laundered pink linen, there were no candles or coloured lights or music. Most of the other diners seemed to be Italian, as were the waiters, and the smell coming from the kitchen was rich and appetising.

I had felt rather tense about going to a restaurant with Nick. Because he usually behaved in his own anarchic way I wasn't sure what I was in for. I did hope he wouldn't put the toy frog on the tablecloth. Just for once, I wanted to be thoroughly conventional. He hung up the crash-helmets and helped me off with the quilted Indian jacket I wore on the bike. 'I couldn't tell you in front of your mother,' he said, 'but you look terrific. She'd have started a moan about how terrific she would have looked if only she'd married the conductor.'

'Too right!' I agreed.

'For two, sir?' the waiter enquired, and Nick said, 'Yes, please.' When we had sat down he nodded generally at my clothes and said, 'Did you make all that lot?'

'Yes, I make most things,' I said. 'It's so much cheaper. I've nearly finished your shirt, by the way.' The tape measure was still in my bag from the time in the park when I had measured his chest and shoulders, arms and collar size. I had loved that lunchtime, prodding him with the metal end of the tape measure and ordering him to turn round or put his arms out sideways.

'What you smiling at?' he asked; but his interest was immediately diverted to the food when the waiter brought the menus. I ordered *prosciutto* and melon to start with but Nick said he hated meat and fruit together and opted for fresh sardines. Absurdly, I wished I had chosen the same as him, not because I liked sardines but because sharing the same tastes made us seem a little closer. He said he wanted chicken to follow but I began to feel worried about the prices and settled for *lasagne*. I knew Nick was earning quite a good wage at the garage but this meal was a lot for him to pay for, specially as he owed money to one or two people. I wouldn't ask him for the ten pounds for the boots.

Nick ordered white chianti. He tasted it when the waiter poured a little into his glass, and nodded. 'Fine,' he said. Although I didn't want to feel surprised, I had to admit that I was relieved at the way he seemed so assured. 'Do you eat out a lot?' I asked. He looked at me and I blushed, knowing

87

he understood why I asked the question. 'Had this rich girl friend didn't I?' he said. 'I was working for this firm that did sports cars and we had to take a Porsche up to this bird's house. At least, it was her father's place but anyway, there she was, rolling in money and bored stiff. I sent her up rotten and she loved it. I suppose nobody had ever talked to her like that before. Anyway, we got together and she took me around everywhere. I had a whale of a time, then I began to feel as if I was a sort of handbag or something, so I shoved off.'

I nodded and smiled understandingly, trying not to feel jealous. He was wearing a shirt with a collar tonight, white, with a pale fawn stripe. His hair always went more curly when he'd just washed it, and I couldn't help thinking how handsome he was. I loved looking at him in new surroundings. It was almost as if I was seeing him for the first time all over again.

The food was delicious. 'All right?' he asked, looking up over his sardines. 'Wonderful!' I said. I felt like singing, which is a mad sensation when you're eating melon and ham. 'I'm so happy!' I told him.

'Well, that's all right, then,' he said, and I thought that I must be careful. He didn't like to hear too much about the way I felt. I had understood by then that he wanted me to be as funny and outrageous as I looked. And nothing else. He didn't want to know about anything 'heavy', as he called it.

In the pause between courses I gazed idly round the room, looking to see if anyone was wearing anything interesting. A large group of Italians sat near us at two tables put together, the men in dark jackets, the women disastrously dressed in thick skirts and short-sleeved tops which emphasized their fat arms. I looked beyond them to the further room which led off the one we were sitting in through a broad arch. I noted a slim woman in a coffee-coloured dress in a linen-textured fabric, finely pleated into a low-cut yoke. She had dark hair, thick and wavy. She reached a bare arm across the pink tablecloth to touch the hand of the man who sat opposite her, and I felt my face burn with shock. The man was my father.

'What's the matter?' asked Nick. 'You look as if you've

seen a ghost.' I didn't know what to say. I was terribly afraid
I was going to cry. 'What *is* it?' Nick insisted. I took a sip of
wine and gave a little laugh. 'Matter of fact, I've just seen my
father over there,' I said lightly. I was going to add, 'With his
girl friend,' but somehow I couldn't say it.

Nick was rather annoyed. 'Bloody marvellous,' he said.
'Take a girl out for a meal and fetch up with her old man as
well. Where is he?'

'Over there,' I said, indicating with my head but not
looking. I didn't want to see him.

Nick stared. 'Baldish, with bushy hair round the edge?' he
asked.

'That's right,' I said, still not looking.

'Oh,' said Nick after a minute or two. 'I see what you
mean. She's not a Bank customer, is she. Or if she is, they're
not here to discuss her investments.'

The waiter appeared. '*Pollo*?' he enquired. 'For me,' said
Nick. He was looking at me rather anxiously. 'And the *lasagne*
for you, signora,' said the waiter. 'Some cheese?'

'Thank you,' I said automatically as he sprinkled grated
Parmesan for me. I was determined not to be upset.

'You can't blame him,' said Nick as he set about his
chicken. 'I mean, most blokes are like that.'

'Don't talk about it,' I said. I didn't want to think about
Mum sitting at home. He takes a real interest in his customers,
she had said proudly. Oh, yes. Not customers. Customer.
And he took a real interest in her. Not half.

I wished I hadn't chosen *lasagne*. It was very nice, but it
was hot and thick and heavy and somehow I didn't feel
hungry any more. My dad, with some other woman. Some
stranger. And Mum all alone. I felt as if I had gone home and
found a big hole where the house used to be. He wasn't my
father any more. He was just some middle-aged man taking
a bird out. A wave of anger swept across me. I put my fork
down and drank some wine.

'You don't want to be upset about it,' Nick said. 'Just
because he's your dad it doesn't mean he can't be a real bloke
with a life of his own. I mean, your mum's not a lot of fun, is

she?'

'Fat lot of chance she gets,' I said. And yet Nick was right. Did *I* enjoy staying in with Mum every night? No. I ate a bit more *lasagne*, furiously trying to get my thoughts straight. I was such a fool. I shouldn't have come here, to a restaurant he had mentioned, on a night when he was out. I might have known I'd meet him. But, to be honest, I hadn't minded the idea of meeting Dad. There had been several little daydreams where Nick and I had met my father with another business acquaintance, a suave man, dark-suited, sophisticated, who would have raised an eyebrow and made some comment along the lines of, 'So you have a girl-about-town for a daughter, David.' And my father would have given me a smile of complicity, thinking back to his own young days when he owned a Norton. Before he met my mother.

'Oh, come on, cheer up,' said Nick impatiently. 'It's not the end of the world.'

I smiled at him. 'Of course it's not,' I agreed. But I couldn't finish the *lasagne*.

When the waiter came he said, 'Something wrong?' and looked at my plate in a concerned sort of way. 'No, no, it's lovely,' I said. 'I just wasn't very hungry.' He made no further comment, but enquired, 'Something else for you? The sweet trolley?'

'Yes, please,' said Nick cheerfully.

I didn't want anything else to eat but I stared at the fruit tarts and *gâteaux* and trifles dutifully as the waiter stood with poised fork and spoon. Then I saw a look of alarm come over Nick's face as he glanced past me. Looking over my shoulder, I saw that my father and the woman were standing up. Her face was turned towards him as he held the jacket, which matched her dress, so she could slip her arms into it. She took the handbag which he passed her and then they came towards us on their way out of the restaurant. He, with his hand under her elbow, was not looking our way, but I was thrown into total panic. I could not face the idea of confronting him. There was no hope of bolting for the Ladies – the waiter and the sweet trolley blocked my escape route. I put my hand to my nose as if afflicted by sudden snuffles and muttered something about needing a hanky. I bent down for my handbag which was on the floor beside my chair, and remained doubled-up as I grovelled needlessly about. I knew the waiter thought I was mad, but I couldn't help that. Peering covertly past Nick's legs, I saw my father and the woman go out so I straightened up, blowing my nose elaborately. Nick had chosen a chocolate *gâteau* and the waiter was looking at me patiently. 'I'll have a *crème caramel*, please,' I said, because it seemed the smallest and easiest thing to eat.

When the waiter had gone I said, 'They didn't see me, did they?'

'Not a chance,' said Nick. 'Far too interested in each other. They wouldn't have noticed if you'd dropped dead on the carpet.'

'Thanks a bunch,' I said gloomily.

In fact, since Dad and the woman had left the restaurant I felt quite a lot better. We stayed for a long time drinking coffee then walked through the Soho streets reading the postcards in shop windows that advertised French lessons and massage, and trying to get a glimpse of the strip shows. Being with Nick in that slightly sinister place made me feel wonderfully safe. Liz and I had walked through Soho once or twice, but always with the prickly sense of being looked at and feeling a little vulnerable.

At last we got on the bike and went home. As we approached the house I was wondering whether Dad was back yet, and if so, what I could say to him. I couldn't let on that I had seen him. And yet to say anything else was a kind of lie. I started to rehearse in my mind the pantomime of appearing normal. 'Yes, we had a lovely time, thank you. Did your business meeting go well?' Could I sound innocent? I doubted it. I would never feel the same about him again.

But he wasn't in. As Nick silenced the bike's engine I could hear the sound of the piano floating out from the house and knew Mum was still alone. She never played when Dad was in.

'You coming in for coffee?' I asked Nick. He shook his

head. 'Better not,' he said. 'Don't want another dose of how lonely she's been.'

'You're a coward,' I accused him.

'Oh, yes,' he agreed happily. 'I'm not sticking my neck out. No point in looking for trouble.' And there was trouble enough, I thought bitterly. He didn't want to get involved.

There was a laburnum tree by the front gate and its dangling leaves made a patch of shadow under the street lamp. The piano tinkled on as we kissed. Mum played Chopin rather slowly, in a particular way which somehow expressed her sigh and her oft-repeated lament that her fingers were stiff these days. But the sweet tune was familiar to me from childhood and now it seemed almost unbearably sad as I listened to it in the street, hurrying my furtive kissing because my father might see us at any moment when he returned home from his own furtive affair.

'I must go,' I said, trying to free myself although I would have loved to stay out there with Nick, all night under the stars.

'Mm,' he said, making no attempt to release me.

'It's been a marvellous evening,' I said.

He kissed me again and said, 'Glad you enjoyed it.' Then he added, 'Pity about your old man. Put you off your nosh a bit, didn't it?'

I freed myself, suddenly panic-stricken at the thought that Dad might come towards us along the pavement at any minute. I glanced over my shoulder anxiously but the street was still empty. 'I really don't want to see him,' I said. 'Not tonight, anyway. I'd better go in.'

Nick shrugged his shoulders. 'All right,' he said. 'If that's how you feel. But you'll have to learn to live with it. See you tomorrow?'

'In the park,' I said. 'And don't be late!'

He grinned, making no promises, gave me a last kiss and put his crash helmet on. I didn't wait to see him get on the bike but ran down the side way to the back door. It seemed desperately important to get away from Dad.

I put my head round the sitting-room door and said, 'Hello,

Mum – just to let you know I'm back.' The music stopped in mid-phrase as she turned from the piano, holding up her hands like a mouse interrupted in washing its face. 'Oh, hello, dear,' she said. 'Would you like a cup of tea?'

'No, thanks,' I said. 'I'd better get straight to bed. Working tomorrow.'

She nodded vaguely and I could see that her head was full of the music. 'All right, love,' she said, and the sad tune began again as I climbed the stairs. But she must have been keeping an eye on the time, for she stopped playing at five past midnight, when the last train came in. A little after that I heard the front gate click as my father returned home.

Chapter 9

When I woke up on Saturday morning I was filled with an urgent feeling that I must get out of the house as quickly as possible, before my father got up. He had become a nightmare figure to be avoided at all costs and I was immensely glad that I had to go to work and so had an excuse to be out of the house.

To my dismay, footsteps sounded on the stairs when I was half-way through a cup of coffee. The kitchen door opened and Dad came in. He looked so rumpled and ordinary that I almost thought I had dreamed the episode last night. It seemed impossible that he was the man who had smiled and raised his glass to the dark-haired woman, and had put his hand under her arm as they went out together. That had been at about half-past eight. And he had not come home until midnight.

'Off to work, love?' he asked.

I said, 'Yes,' and took my coffee to the sink to add some cold water so that I could finish it quickly.

'Your mother says you were out to dinner last night,' he went on. 'Did you go somewhere nice?'

In the ordinary way, I would have told him all about it, but I just said, 'Yes, it was fine, thanks.' I prayed he would not ask me where I went. He looked at me in some surprise because I was so curt, then plugged the electric kettle in and switched it on. I didn't mean to say anything else to him but I heard myself asking in a cynical voice, 'And how was *your* evening?'

'Oh, pretty routine,' he said easily. 'These things get to be a bit of a bore. Where did you go?'

Liar, I thought. Cool, smooth liar. And you are my dad. 'A place in Soho,' I said dangerously, and he looked cautious.

94

'It's a pretty tough area,' he said. 'I don't much like the thought of you being about there.'

I bet you don't, I said to myself. I couldn't find any way to answer him so I gulped down the last of my coffee and said, 'Must go.' Then I picked up my bag and went out.

I was raging inwardly all the way to the shop. How could he lie to me so blatantly and so easily? I supposed it was a habit now. He must have been doing it for years.

In the little room behind the shop I looked in the mirror and realised that the way I had put on my make-up that morning reflected the way I felt. A slapdash fury had overtaken me, for maroon shadow extended to my eyebrows and my eyes were tragically ringed with a heavy-handed black. I was just about to tone it down a bit when Mr Biggs came in. He took his glasses off and put them on again, which was always a bad sign with him.

'Sasha,' he said, 'I have decided with some reluctance to seek an alternative trainee. I am quite willing to give you a reference to the best of my ability under the circumstances, but I really feel that someone of – well – less flamboyant style would be more suitable for this shop. I must therefore give you one week's notice as from today. Your employment with us will terminate next Saturday.'

It was a shock but I tried not to seem upset. I said, 'You mean I've got the sack?'

He avoided the word. 'I am giving you a week's notice,' he repeated. 'I am sincerely sorry that this had to happen.'

'I might as well go now,' I said bleakly. The thought of working for a whole week when they knew I'd got the sack was awful.

'You have already been paid for today,' he pointed out. 'Your further week will of course be paid for next Friday and it will give you a chance to find alternative employment during that time.'

'Oh, big deal,' I said. 'And why are you sacking me, anyway? I haven't been late or anything, not since you said.'

'You were ten minutes late back from your lunch-break

yesterday,' said Mr Biggs primly. 'I'm afraid I never make idle threats.'

I blew up. 'Have a heart! I was ten minutes late going, wasn't I? Because of that stupid woman with odd feet.'

'I am afraid I cannot enter into any discussion of the matter,' said Mr Biggs. He went out and shut the door behind him with a firm, precise click.

Nick didn't come to the park. I waited and waited, sitting there on our bench long after I should have been back at the shop, though I didn't care much since I'd got the sack. I so badly wanted to tell Nick about losing my job. I was sure he said he only worked until one on Saturdays. I trailed miserably back to the shop and was glared at by Mrs Marshall, though she didn't say anything. I almost wished she had. It would have been a relief to have a row with somebody.

Nick didn't come to the shop when we closed. I went along to Ron's and sat there for nearly an hour drinking the coffee which tasted like the smell of a cardboard box and reading the same magazine I had bought nearly a week ago, and trying to avoid Ron's eye. I knew he would say something when I went out alone and I began to pray that Nick would come, if only to release me from sitting there in the corner of a bench seat with my bag beside me and the horribly familiar pages of the magazine on the table in front of me. Every time the door opened I looked up and then looked away again quickly because I didn't want to meet a stranger's eye.

It was nearly quarter to seven. I couldn't sit there all evening. And besides, a fat man in a tee shirt had come to sit opposite me. I turned sideways to stop his knees nudging mine under the table, but he was looking me up and down as he munched his way through sausages and chips, and I knew he was going to say something when he had finished eating. I pushed the magazine into my bag and got out my purse to pay for the coffee. I stood up – and Nick came through the door.

'Hello,' he said casually. 'Fancy you being here. Working late, were you?'

Ron overheard him. Swishing a cup in the sink, he said, 'She's been waiting over an hour for you, mate. More than you deserve.'

'Treat 'em rough,' said Nick. 'They love it, really. Two coffees, two biscuits.'

'*Please*,' said Ron.

'And make it one, not two,' I said. My voice sounded shaky. 'I'm fed up with sitting in here.' I put the money for my coffee on the counter and made for the door. Nick caught me up on the pavement and said, 'Hey, what's the matter?' I was walking fast and he capered beside me, waving his arms as if I was a runaway horse. 'Stop, stop!' he shouted. 'Help! She's gone mad!'

I kept walking. It must look awfully funny, I thought, and I began to cry. He caught me by the arm. 'Sasha,' he said. 'What is it? Come here. Do *stop*, you idiot.' I found myself crying against his chest, with his arms round me. I tried terribly hard to stop because I knew he wouldn't like it.

'Have you got a hanky?' I gulped, but he said in a silly voice, 'Left me handbag in the Ladies, ducky.' I laughed in the middle of my tears and found a Kleenex and blew my nose.

'I must look a fright,' I said.

'Absolutely horrible,' he agreed. We walked on slowly, side by side, and I had the wet Kleenex clutched in my hand. I kept staring at the ground because I knew I must look such a mess and I didn't want to anyone to see my face. We went into the park and sat down on the first bench we came to, not our usual one under the tree but a rather dreary one that faced the litter-strewn football pitch. 'What's it all about?' he asked. He was rolling a cigarette.

'I lost my job,' I said. 'And I waited ages in the park at lunchtime but you didn't come. And I was ages in Ron's with that fat bloke trying to nudge me with his knees under the table, and I keep thinking about Dad and that woman –'

'Look,' said Nick, 'don't get all heavy. I went down the pub with Gary at lunchtime, right? And we had a couple of good ideas about the Triumph so we went round to my mate's

97

place to have a look at it.'

I nodded. 'I'm sorry,' I said miserably. And yet, I didn't see why I should apologise. Wasn't I allowed to tell him the way I felt? Was it my fault that he had not turned up at the park and so increased my load of anxiety?

'Shame about the job,' he said. 'Bet it was the blue-haired old bag. She never liked you, did she?'

'Not a lot,' I said. I found my mirror and set about repairing my make-up while I explained about being late back but how it didn't really count because I'd only had an hour since leaving the shop.

'They'll find any excuse if they're gunning for you,' he said. He watched me while I put on some more mascara and I wondered if he was going to suggest that I looked for a part-time job so we could go to the flat at lunchtimes. But he didn't say anything. It was rather a relief in a way. The thought of going to a Dettol-smelling clinic and explaining to a stranger that I intended to have sexual intercourse had been nagging at me constantly and the more I thought about it the worse it seemed. It was so personal that I could hardly admit even to myself that I wanted to sleep with Nick, specially in a well-organised, deliberate sort of way. It would have been so much easier to be swept off my feet. Some wild, magic evening that ended in moonlight and seduction was easy to imagine; a pre-planned daytime experience was something entirely different. Perhaps Liz and I were kidding ourselves when we said the first time with anyone should be special and marvellous. Perhaps it wasn't like that.

I stared at a Coke can lying at my feet as I pushed the make-up things back into my bag. The can had been folded in half and I thought of the blow with the side of the hand, the triumphant crushing and folding, displaying and discarding, which had left it like that. So many boys couldn't throw a can away without first deforming it.

The football pitch was horrible. It was no better, I thought, when squads of shouting young males opposed each other, struggling to gain a theoretical victory which meant nothing. Beyond it, the trees interlaced with the sky and offered an uncommenting simplicity which was a kind of comfort. But a grief welled up in me because there was so little in which to believe; getting involved in human affairs needed such strong defences against being hurt.

'You're quiet,' said Nick. I nodded, looking at the trees with their leaves turning yellow. Although the afternoon was still warm there was a mistiness about the blue sky which betrayed the fact that the summer was dying. 'It's so sad,' I said.

Nick looked puzzled. 'What is?' he asked.

I had been sitting very still on the bench and I felt as if my bones were filled with lead. I would never move again for the weight which anchored me. 'Everything,' I said. Even my eyes did not move. 'The way things are.'

'Things are the way you want them,' said Nick. 'Give or take a quid or two.'

I did not answer him. The meshing of the trees with the sky was too sad, the football pitch too dreadful.

After a while he said, 'What we going to do tonight, then?'

For a few moments I thought I would do nothing. I would sit there on the bench until I simply stopped existing. Then that dream, too, crumbled. I turned my head to look at him and everything was different. 'Anything you like,' I said.

'Go down the Plumbers?' he suggested.

'Which one's that?'

'Plumbers Arms? The place we went when we came back from Westerham. Gary said he'd be down there.'

I wished I had the strength of mind to say I'd stay at home and watch the telly. I knew what it would mean if Gary was there. He and Nick would discuss motor bikes all evening. And Liz would be at work, so I'd have no-one to talk to. But I couldn't stay at home. Not with my father in the house. So I smiled and said, 'Yes, fine.' He took one last drag on his thin cigarette then dropped it on the grass and trod on it.

When Liz came round on Sunday morning she was a lot more sympathetic than Nick had been when I told her about losing my job.

'Rotten sods,' she said. 'Never mind, love. You'll find something else.'

I shook my head. I felt very depressed this morning. Yesterday evening had been just as boring as I had expected and Nick was not like the person I had gone out with on Friday night. He seemed to be almost flaunting the fact that I adored him, teasing me in front of Gary as if pushing me to the point where I would accept any insult. Sometimes I had given him a cheeky answer but at heart I was sick with the fear of losing him and so I tried to please him to an extent which I would have found nauseating in anyone else. During the evening I had realised that he had not meant to ask me out. Had it not been for my long wait in Ron's he would not have seen me and he and Gary would have been on their own. Once again I had made a fool of myself by letting Nick see too much of my feelings.

'You've got it all wrong about Nick,' said Liz, peering into the mirror as she pulled a wisp of hair through a pad of cotton wool held in the other hand. She had decided to give herself highlights.

I said, 'What do you mean?'

'Your Nick,' she declared, 'needs treating rough. He won't ever take anyone seriously until he meets a girl who can give him the run-around instead of the other way about. Perhaps that's what he's looking for. He saw you with your pink hair and thought, there's a girl who doesn't give a damn for anybody. Little did he know you're such a softy.'

'Little did *I* know,' I said gloomily.

'I should get tough with him if I were you,' advised Liz. 'If he goes off with someone else – well, he probably would have done anyway. This stuff seems awfully strong,' she added, looking at the bottle, 'I do hope these wispy bits don't drop off. How was Friday and the meal up West, by the way? Did you have a good time?'

Friday came flooding back. I had been so busy telling Liz all about losing my job and about the dreary evening with Gary and Nick that the nightmare of Friday had remained untold.

'Poor old you,' Liz said when I had finished. 'Not your week, is it? Are you sure she was a girl friend? I mean, some men are terrifically courteous to a woman they're taking out, even if it is business. Specially old-fashioned blokes like your father.'

I was tempted to try and believe her. It would be so nice to return to thinking of my father as just Dad. Not a traitor, not a two-faced, ugly presence to be avoided at all costs. I had such a sense of loss when I thought about Dad. But it was no use pretending. His face had been alive with interest when he looked at that woman; he seemed like a young man again, as familiar and yet as different as a photograph taken years ago. I shook my head. 'Thanks for trying,' I said, 'but it wasn't business. No way.'

'Have you told him about losing your job?' asked Liz.

'I told Mum,' I said. 'She started on at me for coming home late for supper after I'd been waiting for Nick all that time and had such a dreadful day, and I just burst into tears. The funny thing was, she seemed really annoyed. Not with me, with the shop. Said they hadn't given me a proper chance and then went on about how they probably wanted some mousy little thing that wouldn't say boo to a goose. She's so funny, the way she seems to think she's a a cut above the average. She expects me to be something special, too, and yet she doesn't like it if I am. You can't win.'

'At least she didn't throw a fit,' said Liz. 'Did you tell your Dad?'

'No,' I said. 'I've been keeping out of his way. I can't bear to look at him.'

Liz said, 'Oh, come off it.' She frowned into the mirror, holding up a wisp of hair between finger and thumb. 'Is that light enough, do you think?'.

I didn't really care, but I said, 'They want to be almost white if they're going to show up. And you don't have to be so superior. How would you feel if it was *your* dad?' And then I wished I'd kept my mouth shut.

'Chance would be a fine thing, wouldn't it?' said Liz.

'I'm sorry,' I said, mentally kicking myself. 'Stupid.'

'Oh, I don't mind,' said Liz. 'What you never have, you never miss.' She turned away from the mirror. 'Look,' she said, 'there's something we've got to sort out. What about this holiday?'

I felt as if she was hustling me. The holiday was a lovely idea but the reality of making it happen was fraught with all sorts of difficulties.

'What about it?' I asked rather irritably.

'Well, quite a few things,' Liz sounded cautious. 'It's three weeks since we thought of it. If you're going back to the Sixth Form we'll have to make it the week after next, or term will start.'

'If I went to Aldeburgh with the parents we wouldn't be back until four days into the term,' I reminded her. 'So the same can apply to us.'

'Neither here nor there,' Liz said. 'The main thing is, do you really mean to come? Have you got enough money and have you told your parents – and are you willing to leave Nick?'

The answer to all these questions was no, but I hesitated. I still wanted to think about our holiday and believe it would happen. 'Do you have to know now?' I asked.

'Well, yes, I do really,' said Liz. She looked away. 'Thing is, Gary's got a couple of weeks off in September and his sister works as an *au pair* in Sweden. Do you remember her? Jenny. She left school when we were in the third year.'

'No,' I said.

Liz ploughed on. 'Well, Jenny says the family she works for are quite happy for Gary to go over there and see her – and I can go, too, if I want.'

I said, 'Oh. That's that, then.'

'No, it isn't,' Liz insisted. 'If you want to stick to our plan, we'll go. I'm due two weeks' holiday and Mr Mandel doesn't mind when I take it after the end of next week because the pastry chef will be back then. But I don't want to say no to Gary and then find that you're not coming either.'

I could see her point. It wasn't even unexpected. I had asked her right at the beginning if she was going off with

Gary, and she had said no. At the time, she had meant it. Then something else struck me.

'Liz,' I said, 'if you're going on holiday with Gary, will you –' The question remained unasked, because Liz nodded casually. 'Yeah,' she said. ''Course I will.'

Just like that. The room was quiet in the sunshine. Liz said impatiently, 'You don't have to look so stricken. It was bound to happen sooner or later.'

After a pause I said, 'And was it special?' She shrugged and looked away, then met my eye with a rather sad smile. 'It's not like that,' she said. 'It's just something you do.'

'Yes, of course,' I said quickly. I felt left behind. Left out, left over. I went and stared out of the window at the neatly striped lawn which my father must have cut yesterday when I was at work. I was glad he wasn't out there now, walking up and down behind the lawnmower. Glad, glad. Tears welled up in my eyes.

Liz came and stood beside me, looking out as well. It was funny how we never touched each other. 'Don't be upset,' she said. 'It doesn't make any difference, honestly. I'm still the same.'

I shook my head slowly as the tears spilled over, and cursed myself for behaving like my mother. Liz fetched the box of Kleenex and gave me one. 'I know what you mean,' she said. 'When things happen, they're never what you thought they were going to be.'

I sat down on the window-sill, mopping. 'Sometimes they're great,' I agreed, trying to sound calm. 'But they're never the same. It's as if every time a real thing happens a dream dies.'

'Perhaps it's best not to dream,' said Liz.

After a while we put the old record on and sat side by side listening to the clear voice which had sung so long ago, but I didn't know what Liz's dreams were any more.

When the song ended I said, 'I won't be coming on holiday.'

'Are you sure?' she asked.

I nodded. 'Yes. Quite sure.'

I put on a tango called Jealousy and turned the volume up. I didn't want to talk about it any more.

Nick rang up in the afternoon to ask if I'd like to go to a party that evening. 'Whose is it?' I asked.

'Some bloke I know,' he said vaguely.

Of course I said I would go and he promised to pick me up at eight.

On Sundays Mum always did a roast meal at lunchtime and we had tea in the afternoon. We sat in the dining-room with the French windows open onto the garden. A few early dahlias bloomed by the fence but otherwise it looked rather dull. Squares of sunlight fell across the carpet.

'Sorry to hear about the job, love,' said my father, stirring his tea. I had managed to keep out of his way until now.

'Yes,' I said crisply. 'Pity.'

'Is it worth looking for anything else?' he pursued. 'I mean, we'll be off on holiday before long, and then you'll be back to school.' It would have been the ideal opportunity to broach the subject of going abroad with Liz. How ironic everything was, I thought. But there were still two weeks to fill after I left the shoe shop, even supposing I stayed to work out my notice. 'I'd like to find something else,' I said reluctantly because I didn't want to talk to him. 'It's all experience.'

'Can't argue with that,' said Dad approvingly, glancing across at my mother as if defying her to disapprove. But she was eating a scone and looking out across the grass, and I didn't know what she was thinking, any more than I had known about Liz. It was a very lonely day.

The party was in the block of flats where Nick lived, in a huge estate at the Elephant and Castle. We went up to the twelfth floor in a tin-lined lift that was big enough to put a motor bike in, if not a small car, and pushed open the heavy, brown-painted metal door with reinforced glass panels which led to the corridor outside the front doors of the flats. We could hear the party in full swing.

'Bloody hooligans,' said an elderly man who was approaching us.

''Spect you were a hooligan once, Granddad,' said Nick. 'You're only jealous.'

'Huh!' said the man. But he didn't stay to argue. Nobody argued with a boy Nick's size who wore a leather jacket.

I didn't know anyone at the party. The flat was on two floors with a staircase leading up from just inside the front door, and the centre of activities seemed to be in the upstairs living-room with a kitchen opening off it. As we went in, a boy with a red fez on his head was shaking up a can of beer vigorously. He pointed it at the wall and pulled the ring top then laughed as the frothy beer spurted out in a jet like an aerosol, splashing in a brown stream down the wallpaper. Nick casually took the can out of his hand and pushed him in the chest so that he fell back into an armchair. To my surprise, the boy in a fez made no objection but grinned affably.

'What d'you want to drink?' Nick asked me, and I said recklessly, 'Anything.' The last few days had been so terrible that I felt in the mood for a really good party. I wanted to forget it all and enjoy myself. I did wish there was somebody there I knew.

I was wearing mauve muslin slave trousers and a slinky top made of silver-coloured knitted polyester and a boy in a string vest looked me up and down and said, 'Nice.' He was carrying a bottle of wine by its neck and added, 'Where's your glass?'

'It's okay, thanks,' I said. 'Got one coming.'

'Good,' he said. 'I'll top you up later.' I think he was the host but I never found out for sure.

Nick brought me a glass of something beetroot-coloured. 'Rum and black,' he said. 'Cheers.'

It tasted all right. Quite strong but very fruity, like Ribena with a hiccup.

Nick said, 'Back in a minute – must see a few people.' He disappeared into the crowd and I stood there sipping the rum and black, trying to pluck up the courage to go and talk to someone. Two boys came up and asked who I was. They were both rather good-looking although one of them had the letters of the word LOVE tattooed on the backs of his fingers.

I went with them to the kitchen area which opened off the living-room, in search of another drink. I seemed to have finished the first one rather quickly. I said I wanted rum and black but they couldn't find any rum among the assorted bottles so I had a sweet Martini instead. They filled my glass up to the top, saying, 'May as well get tanked up while it lasts.' There were a lot of crisps in bowls and some bits of cheese on sticks but there didn't seem to be any substantial food. At lunchtime, sitting opposite my father, I hadn't felt hungry. Memories of the *lasagne* in the restaurant somehow got confused with the roast lamb and resulted in a stifled queasiness. It had been the same at tea time and I found that I was now very empty.

The boys, who were called Kevin and Martin, wanted to know if I had brought a friend and I realised that they meant a girl friend. 'Tough luck,' I said. 'I came with Nick Cartwright.' Then I began to wonder where Nick was. I looked round casually and couldn't see him so I topped up my glass intending to go and look for him.

'Pep it up a bit,' said Kevin, tipping a slurp of gin into my Martini.

'Why not?' I said. 'Cheers! See you later.' Then I set out in search of Nick.

All the other rooms on the upper floor turned out to be bedrooms except for the bathroom and loo, and there was no sign of Nick. I went downstairs and looked there. In a room furnished as a bed-sitter I saw him sprawled on a floor cushion with his long legs stuck out before him, rolling a cigarette. A dark haired girl in a printed Indian dress was curled up beside him with her head on his shoulder. They looked as if they had known each other for a very long time. Neither of them noticed me and I went away from the doorway quickly because I didn't want them to see me looking.

I was absolutely determined not to cry. Not in front of all these people. My hands felt clammy. I hated dark-haired women. I went boldly back to the kitchen for another drink. A lot of the bottles were empty now and there didn't seem to be much except red wine or party cans of beer. I chose red wine. I found a bowl containing peanuts and used cocktail sticks, and ate a few nuts. An African girl, with her hair in dreadlocks, came and looked in the bowl and said, 'Mean with the food, aren't they? I do like food at a party.' She wandered off again.

Martin and Kevin came up with a giggling blonde girl in pink Bermuda shorts and suggested we went on somewhere else, but I said I couldn't. I wished I had the courage to go with them and leave horrible, treacherous Nick to look for me in vain at the end of the evening, but I didn't want to be part of a foursome which would involve a pairing-off with either Martin or Kevin. I wished I didn't care about Nick. I wished I could feel a part of the party but I was looking at it as an outsider, terribly alone.

'You don't seem to be having much fun,' said Kevin kindly. In preparation for departure he had put on a huge ex-RAF great-coat, and he fished in the pocket and produced a half bottle of whisky. 'What you need is a proper drink,' he said. 'Here.' And he topped up my glass of red wine from his whisky bottle. 'See you,' he said. 'I expect we'll be back.' And they went out.

I knew I shouldn't drink a mixture of red wine and whisky, specially after rum, Martini and gin. But I didn't care. If Nick could behave badly, so could I. And what was a party for, anyway? I ate one or two rather ashy crisps and drank some more of the poisonous mixture, noticing vaguely that nothing seemed to have much taste any more. I was very thirsty. I drank some more. Who did Nick think he was, anyway? Liz was right. Must get tough with him.

I set off in search of Nick. He wasn't in the room with the floor cushion. I went from room to room. One of the doors was locked but I thought it was probably somebody's private room which they didn't want invaded. Could Nick have gone without me? Surely not. But the thought was frightening. I found the boy in a string vest and asked him if he had seen Nick.

'He's around,' he said vaguely. 'Probably in the loo. Have you got a drink?'

'Yes, thanks,' I said gaily. Must be tough. He topped my glass up again, this time with white wine. What the hell. In the loo. Hadn't thought of that.

'There's two loos,' the boy called cafter me. 'Upstairs and down!'

'Thanks!' I called back. It seemed difficult to turn my head.

The upstairs loo was empty. I made my way carefully down to the other one, and found the door locked. I waited outside it. He had to be in here if he hadn't gone off on the bike. Unless he was behind the locked bedroom door. No. There was no point in imagining things. That was simply somebody's bedroom which was locked because they didn't want it messed about.

A girl in a red dress with white coin dots on it came out and held the door open for me. 'Sorry,' she said. 'Were you waiting?'

Automatically, I went in. And it was then, shut in the little cell with the lavatory bowl staring at me like a huge white eye, that I realised I was drunk. Everything wheeled round me when I shut my eyes. Better keep eyes open, I said seriously. Mustn't stay shut in here. Probably giving me claustrophobia. That was it. That's why I felt so bad.

I opened the door and was almost fallen on by the boy in a red fez, who was waiting impatiently to get in.

'Claustro - phobia,' I told him carefully. It was a very difficult word to say.

'Gerraway?' he said with polite interest, and unzipped his trousers, elbowing the door shut behind him.

I was more thirsty than ever. I drained the glass in my hand but the liquid in it didn't seem wet. Must find Nick. Upstairs. Stairs lurching. Like on a ship, going to Switzerland, school ski-ing trip. Stairs lurching. Flat lurching. Whole blasted block lurching. Good sailor, though.

Top of the stairs, locked door.

Then it opened. Nick. Dark-haired girl behind him, holding his arm, smiling up. Like that woman with Dad. Nick saw me. Stopped smiling. 'Oh, hello. Having a good time?' But his face uneasy. Guilty.

I remember trying to say, 'I'm a good sailor,' because every-thing was so unsteady, and I remember the girl saying sar-castically to Nick, 'You do pick some funny friends, darling.' And then they were all trying to drag me away from her. The dark hair was in my face, the condescending smile under my fingernails. There was screaming and confusion. The ceiling slid across where the wall had been. They were carrying me. Everything plunged about. Something was pressing all along my side. A bed. I was lying down. Nick's face was in front of me. He said, 'Take it easy. You don't want to get upset.'

I tried to say, 'Having a good time,' but suddenly my face felt cold and clammy and my throat tightened. 'Going to be sick,' I said. He hauled me to my feet. I took a few steps then started to vomit. I pressed my hands over my mouth desper-ately but it was no good. 'Sink,' said somebody, and I found myself being sick into a stainless steel sink that was half-full of dirty glasses standing in greasy washing-up water.

'Oh, God,' I said, and was sick again.

I don't remember much of what happened after that. I think I was asleep. Then I was in the back of a car and I kept asking where Nick was. There were other people in the car but I didn't know who they were and in a while the car stopped and they opened the door. The air felt very cold and I was shivering. We stood on a doorstep banging at the knocker and ringing the bell and I realised it was my house and I couldn't understand why we didn't go round the back. I tried to say so but it all seemed too difficult. Then the door opened and my mother stood there in her dressing-gown. She looked at me and said, 'Oh, *Susan!*'

There were voices arguing downstairs and the sheets felt chilly. I put my hands out to the edge of the bed to try and stop it rocking about but the awful lurching went on and on.

Chapter 10

When I woke the next morning I felt very ill. I ached all over and my stomach hurt. The daylight blazing in through the curtains attacked my eyes painfully when I opened them and my head throbbed as I turned away from the light. God, I thought, I've got to go to work. I tried to sit up but the room rocked. I lay down again and pulled the sheet over my face. It was slightly less awful in the dark.

'Susan,' said somebody. I struggled awake again. It was Mum.

'Wasser time?' I asked. It was difficult to talk because my mouth felt as if it was full of fur.

'Quarter-past one,' said Mum.

I said. 'Oh, no.' Mr Biggs would think I had left.

'Well, it doesn't matter, does it,' said Mum, 'since you've got the sack.' I hadn't told her I was supposed to do one more week. 'What on *earth* were you doing last night?' she asked. 'Here. I've brought you a cup of tea.'

'Thanks,' I said thickly. I sat up. Pain stabbed through my head. I wasn't sure if I could drink the tea.

Mum said, 'Who were those people who brought you home?'

'I don't know,' I said. I was desperately thirsty but I still felt sick.

Mum sighed. 'I suppose everyone has to find out the hard way, but I must say I think you've been very stupid. It's not as if you're a complete stranger to drinking. We always let you have a glass of wine if we'd opened a bottle with a meal, it seemed so much more civilised. And a sherry before dinner and –'

'Don't,' I said. 'Please don't talk about alcohol.' I took a cautious sip of tea.

110

'I can't think what Nick was doing to let you get into such a state,' Mum went on. 'I know he's a bit of a rough diamond but I thought he was quite a nice boy at heart.'

That's where you're wrong, I thought dismally. Nick's a cruel boy at heart. Like a re-run video tape I saw him come out of the bedroom with the dark-haired girl. The sip of tea began to jump in my stomach. Mum looked at me and said, 'I'll get a bowl.' But I couldn't wait for her to get back from the kitchen. I rushed into the loo and stood there heaving and heaving, though I was too empty to be sick and my stomach felt as if it was going to tear in half. I swore that I would never, never drink anything again.

The next day I simply felt as if I had 'flu, which was quite a lot better. I got up very late and Mum said she was making scrambled eggs on toast. To my surprise, I found that I was ravenously hungry although I still ached. Over lunch I said, 'I'm awfully sorry about Sunday. I didn't drink all that much but it was such a silly mixture.'

'Fatal,' she said. She buttered another piece of toast and offered it to me and I said, 'Thanks.' Somehow it was rather nice to be having lunch with Mum again. It felt very safe and cosy although I knew I wouldn't want to go on doing it for long.

'Everyone gets drunk sooner or later,' Mum said. 'I remember when I'd been asked to go to some frightfully high-powered reception, I was so nervous that I helped myself rather liberally to the cooking sherry. I didn't realise that we'd be having cocktails somewhere else before we went to this do. By the time we got there I was terribly tipsy. There was a long flight of carpeted stairs, at the top names were being announced and hands shaken, and I caught my foot on the top step and fell flat at my hostess's feet. I've never been so embarrassed.'

'Was that with Dad?' I asked, and she said, 'Oh, no, long before his time.' Her face wore a soft look as she thought back to something private in her own mind.

I became aware of a needling curiosity about my parents. I knew them so well that they were as familiar as the pattern on my bedroom wallpaper; and yet, as adult people who lived their lives in the same way that I lived mine, I hardly knew them at all.

'Mum,' I said, feeling like a surgeon with poised scalpel, 'do you think it matters if people are faithful to each other or not?'

I could see that she was considering this question as it affected me. She was touched to be consulted about her daughter's welfare, specially on such a romantic subject.

'Things are so different these days,' she said, trying to be objective. 'People don't really give each other that kind of understanding, do they? Not unless they are really committed to each other.' She looked at me and added gently, 'Expecting too much is bound to be painful, I'm afraid.'

'But what about married people?' I persisted. 'Does the state of being married really make all that difference?'

'Oh, a tremendous difference,' she said with certainty. 'If you're actually going to *marry* a boy you have to be really sure of him, don't you? You mustn't rush into that sort of thing.'

I said, 'Don't look so worried! I'm not contemplating it. But if I was – do you think marriage vows and all that still really count?'

'Of course,' she said. 'Otherwise there's no point.'

I put my head on one side and tried to sound as if my next question was sheer speculation. 'Supposing Dad was having an affair with someone else? What would you do?' I asked.

'Since he isn't,' she said flatly, 'I don't have to think about it, thank God.'

'But if he was,' I insisted. My imaginary scalpel was tracing a line of blood on the skin. She looked at me very hard.

'I don't know what you're trying to do,' she said, 'but just because your father's work takes him out sometimes in the evenings, there's no need to start imagining things.'

'Purely hypothetical, Mum!' I protested. But her evasion had whetted my appetite and I was hot on the trail of her vulnerability. 'I just wondered what you'd do if you found him out,' I said, ashamed of myself but unable to stop.

'If I really did,' she said after a pause, 'I think I would feel
112

completely betrayed. My life might have been quite different if I hadn't married when I did. I know you can't weigh up things that *didn't* happen as a counter-balance to things that did, because it doesn't work like that. But all the same, considering the potential I threw away, if I found that I hadn't even had his fidelity, I'd feel that it had all been for nothing.'

'A sell-out,' I said.

She nodded and said, 'Exactly.' But she brightened up bravely and added, 'Fortunately, it's not like that.'

'Of course not,' I said heartily, but I couldn't look at her. And the knot of anger against my father, which seemed to be tying up my mind in anguish, took another, tighter turn.

I spent the next day trying to get another job. It was no good. This time there were no cards in shop windows and the woman in the Job Centre didn't even bother with any good advice. I was back to hanging around the shops, killing time, wishing the hours away. I bought a new kind of hair dye, a more mauvy pink, and remembered with a kind of disbelief that in a couple of weeks I would be back at school, with hair returned to its basic mouse colour. It didn't seem possible. I wasn't the same person. I couldn't go back.

I went into the park and sat on the bench where I had so often shared sandwiches with Nick, and wondered if I would ever see him again. Since the party there had been no communication from him. Hurting myself, I pictured him telling the dark-haired girl all the things he had told me; how he didn't want to get involved, couldn't be committed to one person. 'There's a lot of world out there,' he had said, looking across the quiet valley from the churchyard in Westerham. The world was there for me, too, I argued with him silently, it's the same for all of us, you can't use that as an excuse. And nobody can understand you better than I do. Most people wouldn't even see past the act you put on, the leather jacket and the cheerful rudeness. Who else knows the sensitive, uncertain person you really are?

A wind had sprung up and dry leaves blew across the

patchy, littered grass. I waited for nearly two hours, but Nick did not come.

At quarter-to-three I got up and went to Mario's, the restaurant where Liz worked. I went round to the back door which always stood open because the kitchen got so hot, and looked in.

'What you want?' shouted a fat man in a chef's hat through a cloud of steam.

I said, 'Is Liz there?'

He turned his head, gave a piercing whistle through his teeth and shouted, 'Friend wants you. And don't be long.'

Liz came to the door wearing kitchen whites, wiping her hands on a cloth. 'Oh, hello,' she said. 'Of course, it's Early Closing day, I forgot.'

'It's been Early Closing all week for me,' I said. I started to tell her about what had happened at the party but she interrupted apologetically. 'Look we've got an awful rush on,' she said. 'There's a Rotary dinner tonight, so I can't stop now. I've got stuff in the mixer. Ring you later, okay?'

'Okay,' I said, and went away feeling jealous. There was no stuff in my mixer, I thought. Nothing in anything. Blank.

I went home and finished Nick's shirt, stitching on maroon buttons with bitter concentration. It was a successful shirt and I knew he would look marvellous in it. But would he ever wear it? I put the finished garment on a hanger in my wardrobe and shut the door. If he wanted his shirt, I told myself firmly, he could jolly well come and ask for it.

My father came in looking pleased with himself that evening. I was in the kitchen setting the table for Mum and although I cringed inwardly at the sound of Dad coming to the back door, I couldn't just drop the knives and forks and rush out.

'I think I may have found you a job,' he said when he saw me. 'A nice little opening in the rag trade.' He sounded as if he was quoting someone else.

'Oh, yes?' I said coolly, and was painfully pleased to see his frown of hurt perplexity.

'It's a chap called Joss Abraham,' he said, ignoring my

curtness. 'I've known him for years, off and on. Since we were boys.'

'Joss?' said Mum. 'Is he in London, then? I thought he was still up in Yorkshire. We haven't seen him and Myra for years.'

'He's been here for a bit,' said my father guardedly and gave me the ghost of a wink, I wondered what he meant and wished I could ask. I remembered how he always resisted Mum's attempts to organise social meetings with his business friends. 'His son's in the firm now,' he said. 'They're expanding!' He turned to me and went on, 'Joss came in to see me today about some finance for this new venture. He was complaining bitterly that he can't find a girl with a flair for clothes who's prepared to work hard. I told him about you wanting to be a designer and he was most interested. Mind you, I said you'd got to go back to school but he said he wouldn't mind giving you a trial now with a view to future employment if you're interested.'

Interested! It sounded like my dreams come true. I made up my mind in that instant to chuck up school and get into the rag trade. 'I might give it a spin,' I said off-handedly. 'Where does he live?'

'It's nothing much to look at,' my father said. 'Just a little place in a back street in Peckham, but he's got some interest in a mail order firm and he's very well thought of in the trade.' He held out a scrap of paper on which he had written the name and address in his rapid, flyaway scrawl.

I said, 'Thanks. I'll look him up.' As I put the piece of paper under the spaghetti jar on the work top I saw Dad look at my mother with raised eyebrows as if seeking enlightenment on my truculent mood, but she made a face which, together with a slight shrug of the shoulders, said that she, too, was in the dark. Ironically, Mum and Dad talked to each other a lot during supper. Like some kind of sulking, maladroit matchmaker, I seemed to have brought them together. I brooded darkly over the goulash and boiled rice on the few words it would take to drive them apart again; perhaps for ever.

The mauvy pink hair dye was rather subtle, I thought. And at least fiddling about with it last night had given me some respite from the endless grieving over Nick which made life seem so pointless. On Thursday morning I decided to look Russian. Since my high-heeled boots with the wrinkly ankles were the most effective footwear I possessed, there wasn't much choice – they gave everything a faintly Ninotchka look. Because of this the clothes I had made in recent months hovered somewhere between the style of a buttoned-up Tsarina and a Balkan peasant. I wondered what, if anything, would impress Mr Abraham. Was I going to meet a glossy business-man, fat, rich, sophisticated, jetting to Paris and New York and Tokio? I couldn't look suave and well-dressed in the *haute couture* sense of the word.

Finally I put on the high-necked white cotton blouse which had driven me mad with its ambitious plethora of lace and pintucks, and a deeply-flounced brown cotton skirt. It looked absurdly demure with my pinky-lilac hair so I added a black leather belt and a string of amethyst beads my grandmother had given me, and put on my sleeveless quilted jerkin. Looking in the mirror, I wished my hair wasn't pink, after all. A rich chestnut brown would have looked much better with these clothes. But it was too late to change it now. I gave it the scarf and beads treatment and decided that the general effect was much better.

Mum thought otherwise. Meeting me in the hall, she said, 'What *do* you look like? Really, Susan, you –'

'Give it a rest, Mum,' I said. 'I know exactly what I look like and, yes, I am going out like that and, no, I don't care what people think.'

She turned her head away with a hurt lift of the chin, and went into the kitchen. Meanly, I let myself out of the front door without saying goodbye to her. I didn't want the risk of a row before I set out.

Dad's description of a back street in Peckham had sounded picturesque and appealingly squalid but in fact one side of it was open to the sky as a result of redevelopment. New flats stood at intervals along it with grassed-in spaces between them which were neither parks nor gardens. It was no use looking for a tailor's shop over there. I was walking along the unimproved side of the road where the wide pavement was cracked and uneven and the small shops were surmounted by an unbroken three-storey Georgian terrace with small-paned sash windows.

I inspected the shops as I walked past them. A hairdresser with fly-blown display cards advertising out-of-date styles, a betting shop, a greengrocer, a general store with thick wire mesh behind the windows, a do-it-yourself shop with boxes of bathplugs and stick-on tiles standing outside. Then the street began to deteriorate. The next shop was boarded up, then there was a newsagents with sex magazines in the window, an insurance agent, who also seemed to be a small building society, and a very grubby-looking chemist. Then there was a small, dark shop which didn't seem to be a shop at all. There were two dresses on old-fashioned stands in the window, both of them in spotted silk, one navy and white, one red and white. I almost laughed. To my taste, they were impossible clothes, neither ancient enough to be fabulous nor casual enough to be wearable. Their formality was absurd. A small printed card in the frosted glass door announced, 'J. S. Abraham. Tailor and Cutter. High Class Ladies' Wear a Speciality.'

So this was it. My heart sank with disappointment. Trust my father to get it all wrong. I wasn't interested in clothes like those stupid garments in the window. What could I learn in a place like this? I looked at the door and debated whether or not to ring the bell. There was no point in wasting time with a grubby little outfit that could be of no use to me. On the other hand, I had nothing else to do.

As I raised my finger to the bell the door opened. A small, wrinkled woman in a black cardigan over a striped wool dress came out and put an empty milk bottle down on the step. She smiled at me and said, 'Can I help you, my dear?' She had a slight foreign accent.

I found myself explaining who I was and that my father had given me Mr Abraham's address. She put a knobbly-knuckled hand on my sleeve with a kind of sparkling excitement and said, 'Joss will be so pleased! Come in, come in!' Beckoning and patting, she shooed me past her rather like somebody getting a hen into a chicken run, shut the door behind us and said, 'Excuse me while I tell my husband.' Then she went out of a rear door calling, 'Joss! Joss! Where are you?'

I looked round the shop. Old-fashioned glass-fronted shelves lined the wall behind the wooden counter with a brown linoleum top. Obviously the place had at one time been used as a tailor's shop. I could visualise the bales of cloth on the shelves, the pattern books open on the counter. There were even a couple of high bentwood chairs for the customers to sit on while they selected their chosen style. I supposed that in the days before the multiple stores made cheap ready-to-wear clothes universally obtainable, people came to a shop like this to have garments made for them. Now, the only sign of any creative activity was a single evening dress displayed on a dressmaker's dummy with a mahogany handle sticking up out of its neck.

Apart from the wide cowl neckline, the dress was so simply cut that it might have been carved out of stone. It was in grey watered silk and when I went to look at it more closely I realised the astonishing skill of design and construction which resulted in its look of absolute certainty. I suddenly felt that I looked like a walking rag-bag. The dress on the dummy belonged to a standard of professionalism which was completely outside my range.

Chattering voices preceded the return of the small woman, this time chivying a white-haired man in front of her. He, too, was in a cardigan, a drooping, shapeless garment the colour of pea soup worn over baggy-kneed trousers and a shirt of finely striped cotton with no tie. He wore gold-rimmed glasses but, unlike Mr Biggs, he did not snatch them off to shake hands. By tucking in his chin and raising his eyebrows he managed to look over the top of them while shaking my hand in both of his own. I thought for a moment that I was going to hate this affectionate clasp, but I didn't. His hands were

118

hard and warm and I had the extraordinary feeling that I was greeting someone I had known for a long time.

'It's wonderful to see you,' he said. 'We have met before but you won't remember that – I think you were about eighteen inches tall at the time. Come along in, come along.' He turned to the door at the rear of the shop, towing me by the hand. I looked at his wife to see if she minded this familiarity but she smiled at me with equal enthusiasm. Although she was grey-haired her eyelashes were as dark as Nick's, startling in her wrinkled, rag-doll face.

The room behind the shop was tiny, but it was crammed with a weird assortment of things. Most of the floor space was taken up by a heavy mahogany table piled with magazines, books, papers, bits of material, a typewriter, half a loaf on a wooden board, pots containing cherry jam and pickled cucumbers and a large brown teapot and several dirty cups. Bookshelves lined the rest of the room but layers of dresses and fabric samples hung from a row of hooks along the top, obscuring the titles of the stacked and crammed books. The daylight hardly penetrated through intricately patterned net which hung next to the windows, completed by heavy velour curtains on wooden rings. Half-submerged under papers and fabrics was an old-fashioned treadle sewing machine, though I saw that it had been fitted with an electric motor.

'Is this where you work?' I asked.

They both laughed. The woman was putting dirty cups onto a tray with a series of quick snatches.

'No, no,' said Mr Abraham, still chuckling gently, 'one could not work in such a room. A few ideas, yes, a place to relax, have a talk, but a workroom?' He flapped a dismissive hand. 'We have a room upstairs where we make up a toile sometimes but most of the work is done at my son's place now.' Then he smiled at me again. 'What a pretty girl you are, Sasha! David told me you were pretty but every father thinks his daughter is beautiful. Sit down, sit down, my dear. Myra, shall we have some tea?'

His wife was half-way out to the little kitchen which I could glimpse through an open door in the far corner of the room.

'I put the kettle on already,' she called back. Mr Abraham sat down and leaned across the corner of the table to examine my blouse. 'Did you make this?' he asked. I nodded and said, 'I make all my clothes. They're not very good though. Not like that beautiful dress out there.' He did not deny it, but simply asked, 'Do you use patterns?'

'Not for most things,' I said, 'but I do have an old Simplicity pattern for a classic shirt-blouse. I use it as a basis for everything, with different necklines and sleeves. Bit of a cheat, really.'

He was running a professional eye over my clothes, twitching back the edge of my jerkin to look at the lining, turning a cuff button aside to inspect the stitching of the button hole. 'Stand up,' he said, then smiled to soften the order and added, 'You don't mind?'

I did as I was asked, and turned round slowly as he instructed me in the small space in the middle of the cluttered room. I knew there was a slight dip in the hem of my brown skirt, and I knew he would notice it.

'So,' he said, sitting back. 'You have some flair. A good sense of style. Sit down, my dear. Your father says you want to come into this business.' He leaned his folded arms on the table, shoulders hunched. 'How do you see yourself?' he asked. 'Tell me all about it. What are your ambitions?'

I told him how I had always wanted to be a designer and as I talked I remembered the terrible Careers interview at school when I had confided my ambitions to a woman from County Hall in a badly-cut purple tweed suit. She had twirled a pen between her fingers as I talked, then looked at me with a patronising smile and said, 'Yes, but it's not very practical, is it? What are you *really* going to do?'

Mr Abraham was not like that. He sat back and thought about it, pulling at his lower lip between finger and thumb. 'It's a question of which way to set about it,' he said. 'You can stay at school, take your examinations, go to art school, take more examinations, specialise in dress design then hope to get taken on by one of the multiples. A few students make a name for themselves early but it's a matter of luck and

120

backing.'

'Isn't there any other way?' I asked desperately. I had been so sure that I wouldn't go back to school. The decision I had made so instantly seemed predestined.

He looked at me shrewdly and this time he did not smile. 'The other way is all hard work,' he said. 'You would have to learn the trade from the bottom up if you came to us, starting as a machinist. There would be nothing creative for you at first. You would have to learn to be quick and neat, how to do every kind of seam and buttonhole and pocket, how to hand-sew, how to put up with making the same thing again and again. It is very hard; very dull. Not at all glamorous. Badly paid.'

'I wouldn't mind,' I said earnestly. 'I want to do it properly. I want to express my own ideas eventually – of course I do, more than anything. But I don't want people to think I'm just – well – arty.'

He suddenly laughed. 'But my dear Sasha, you *are* arty! Just look at you!' But he put his hand over mine as it lay on the table and added quickly, 'And so you should be. At your age, ideas should be fizzing out of you like soda from a syphon.'

His wife came in with the tea. 'Is it all settled?' she asked as she slid the tray onto the table.

Mr Abraham shook his head at her. 'Always in such a hurry!' he said. But she was not abashed. 'She could start with Bernard,' she urged him. 'You know you need another girl since Rachel went and we need some young ideas, Joss. With Bernard starting the mail order business it won't be *haute couture*, you know. You have to get your finger on the pulse, get the feeling of the young styles!'

Mr Abraham flung his hands in the air and turned to me with comic appeal. 'See what I have to put up with?' he said. 'I try to be the careful business man, play the cards close to my chest as they say, but with Myra? Pouf! All out in the open.'

'Sasha, you want milk or lemon?' asked Myra, unruffled. She had already put a slice of lemon in her own tea and milk in her husband's.

'Lemon, please,' I said, laughing. They were irresistible, these two.

'All right,' said Joss with resignation, helping himself to sugar. 'I'll tell you all about it, Sasha. My father trained me as a tailor like himself and left me his business. I built it up. Did well. Started to branch into women's wear and built up a modest reputation. I had a number of wealthy customers who came to me for all their clothes.'

'Most of them now dead,' put in Myra.

Mr Abraham nodded. 'And the trade died with them,' he said. 'I was slow to realise it. I should have gone into mass production years ago but – ' he shrugged. 'If you are good at something and your customers depend on you, it is hard to change. We moved to London when my cousin Solly died – this used to be his place, you see. I thought it would bring us a bigger market but London had changed even faster. Things were worse here than they were in Leeds. We had a bad time.'

Myra looked at him, shaking her head. 'There is no money in *haute couture* these days,' she said. 'We all told him.'

'There will always be a few rich women who are willing to pay for exclusive clothes,' Mr Abraham said defensively, 'but of course, it's true. The bulk of the money these days is in ready-to-wear. My son, Bernard, understood all this long before I would admit it, and when the time came for him to have a share in the business he wanted to set up a different line. We had disagreements, of course.' Myra rolled her eyes reminiscently but her husband was not to be side-tracked. 'But Bernard was right,' he went on. 'He made me take out a bank loan, found bigger premises, and turned out a larger quantity of stuff, aimed at a younger market. And he's done well.'

'And now he's starting a mail order business?' I asked.

Mr Abraham nodded. 'That's right. His cousin is in it already with micro-chip goods from Taiwan so it's all set up. When the catalogue is ready he'll be in business.' He sipped his tea and looked at me seriously. 'Now, listen,' he said. 'If you work for us you will be treated like the other girls. You will call me Mr Abraham and my son Mr Bernard while we are in the workroom, and you will work very hard, the same as they do. But there will be a difference. We will take you on as an apprentice – if you decide to come to us, that is – and we will train you completely, both on the technical side and in design and cutting.' He thought for a moment and added, 'It may be a good thing if you go on Day Release to an art school for a part of your design training, to keep up with modern ideas. All right so far?'

I nodded enthusiastically.

'There's another side to it,' he went on. 'You can help us with ideas. When we come in here to talk, it is as Joss and Myra and Sasha and Bernard. We all discuss and argue, draw ideas on bits of paper, decide on what we like – and if the idea we choose is one of yours, you will be paid for it. But until such time as you are a qualified designer, while you are our apprentice, any idea of yours that we use will go out under the name of our firm. Is that agreed?'

I said, 'Yes, of course.' I couldn't take it all in straight away.

Myra said, 'You are confusing her, Joss. Listen, Sasha, talk to your father about it, right? He understands this business – he'll be able to advise you.'

I felt my face freeze up. Mr Abraham, who was watching me, said quickly 'Sometimes it's not easy to talk to your family. I'll give him a ring and make sure he approves. If there's one person you musn't upset it's your Bank Manager!'

'Even if he is an old friend,' agreed Myra.

I tried to smile but there was a kind of horror at the back of my mind when I thought about Dad. I didn't know what to say next. There was an awkward silence.

'What happens next?' asked Myra. 'We'll leave it to you, Joss, shall we?'

'Sasha had better give us a try for a day or two and see how she likes it,' said Joss, smiling at me. 'She might decide it's terrible!'

'Couldn't I start now?' I begged.

They both laughed. Mr Abraham looked up at a French

carriage clock on the cluttered mantelpiece and said, 'No, it's nearly lunch-time. But I'll take you to meet Bernard and show you the workrooms. And listen, Sasha, don't wear any trailing scarves or floppy sleeves when you go to work. The machines are very fast. We don't want you to have an accident.' He stood up. 'Are you coming with us, Myra?'

His wife smiled and shook her head. 'I have too much to do,' she said.

The rest of the morning was even more like a dream. The workrooms were ten minutes' walk away, in a building over a garage, as bright as a fish tank because of the big windows and the long glass panels in the roof. Girls sat at wide benches and I saw what Mr Abraham meant about the machines being fast. Unlike the one I was used to, they made a zipping sound rather then a gentle chatter, and the fabric flew under the needles at an alarming rate.

We went into the glass-panelled office at the end of the big room and I was introduced to Bernard, a fat, jolly young man in shirt sleeves who shook hands with the same warmth as his father and looked at me with the amazement I was used to. But Bernard's amazement was different.

'Hey!' he said excitedly. 'Just look at the girl! Exactly what I want!' His father was looking faintly perplexed but Bernard turned to me and asked, 'Have you done any modelling, love? Photographic, I mean. Fashion. Keep your clothes on, all decent.'

I said, 'No, I haven't.'

'Pity Michael isn't here,' he said. 'Could have had a go.' He went to a dress rail and looked me up and down critically over his shoulder, flicking through a row of taffeta dresses on hangers then picking one out. 'This should fit you. Like to try it on?' He pushed the dress at me and I looked round for somewhere to change. 'Ladies' toilet,' he said. 'Round the corner, first right.'

I put the dress on. It was a brilliant sea-green with a close-fitting sleeveless top and a short skirt consisting of four layers of ruffles. Bernard was right. It fitted me perfectly. The scarf and beads which I wore in my hair didn't suit the dress so I took them off and shook out my pink ringlets. Then, feeling terribly self-conscious, I walked back to the office.

'Look at that!' exclaimed Bernard. 'Great, isn't it!' He seemed to talk in a serious of short bursts. 'Turn round, darling. Marvellous. Listen, do you want to model for my catalogue? I'll pay you. Such legs she's got!' he added to his father, who was not looking entirely happy.

'We're not here to talk about photographs, Bernard,' he said. 'I told Sasha we'd take her as a trainee machinist in the first place, with a possibility of signing her up as an apprentice. She wants to be a designer.'

'Don't they all,' said Bernard as he darted round me staring at the dress from various angles. 'I mean, yes, of course we'll take her. Michael's at IPC this week.' He clucked fretfully. 'Pity. Like to get some pictures of this girl.'

'Go and change now, Sasha,' said Mr Abraham mildly. As I left the room I saw him put his hand on his son's shoulder, propelling him gently towards a chair. Obviously he had something to say to him.

When I came back Bernard said politely, 'Come in tomorrow, Sasha, if you want to try the job for a day. Then we'll get something sorted out about a contract and if everyone's happy you can start a full week on Monday. Modelling – well, that's something else. Maybe you'd like to try it one of these days.'

It was all so crazy and marvellous that I began to laugh. 'I'd love to,' I said.

Bernard grinned briefly as he looked at me laughing. 'We start at eight o'clock in the morning,' he said. 'Is that so funny?'

But I couldn't make my face look serious. At that moment I felt on top of the world.

Chapter 11

I went home and told Mum all about it. I had been tempted to go to Mario's and tell Liz, but I knew the restaurant would be busy at lunch-time, and I didn't want to get her into trouble with the chef. He was pretty ferocious, that chef.

Mum had lunch all ready, with mushroom quiche and salad, so I was glad I'd come back, for her sake. I knew what it was like to wait for someone who didn't turn up. She seemed pleased to hear about my plans with the Abrahams but when she realised that I had no intention of going back to school she was dismayed. 'You need the qualifications,' she said. 'What if you change your mind about this job and decide you want to go to university?'

I reminded her that only the other evening she was lamenting that she had made the wrong choice in opting to stay at college instead of going off to Italy with her glamorous boy friend. Confronted with it, she looked unhappy. 'Well,' she said defensively, 'it's easy to interpret it that way afterwards, but how was I to know what would happen at the time? Suppose I *hadn't* met your father?'

'Suppose you *had* gone to Italy,' I countered. 'Of course, you wouldn't have had me. Or perhaps you would. I wonder if I'd still have been me if I'd had a different father? I mean, I wonder if that child would have been a me or a someone else.'

Mum said, 'These sort of questions can't be answered.' She sat in silence for a bit, then she said, 'Susan, what's the matter between you and your father?'

'Nothing!' I said quickly, but I felt a blush of embarrassment creep over my face.

'Yes, there is,' she insisted. 'You've hardly spoken a word to him for the last few days and he's very hurt about it. He asked me if it's anything he'd said.'

'No, of course not,' I said irritably. 'It's just – well, things have been a bit grotty lately, one way and another.'

She frowned. 'I know this will sound silly,' she ventured, 'but after what you said the other day about how I'd feel if David was having an affair, I wondered if you'd got some idea that he was. If that's what was upsetting you. But you would tell me, wouldn't you, if you thought something like that?'

'Yes, of course,' I said wildly. This was awful. What had I done? Why on earth hadn't I kept my big mouth shut? And I had no plans for anything to do all afternoon. If I spent three hours locked in conversation with my mother she was bound to find out what I knew. Or I'd get angry in the effort to hold out against her enquiries and we'd have a row. Before I had consciously worked it out I said, 'I'm just popping out for a bit. I promised Nick I'd let him have that shirt.' It gave me a risky kind of thrill to talk about him in that casual way, as if he was a well-established boy friend. As if he was any kind of boy friend.

Mum gave a faint sigh. 'Oh,' she said. 'Well, if you must.'

I offered to stay and help with the washing-up but she shook her head in a resigned sort of way. 'It'll give me something to do,' she said.

I wrapped the shirt in tissue paper and put it in a carrier bag, then set out. Bennett's Garage was down a side road just past the cinema. It wasn't a big place with self-service pumps. There was no canopy over the forecourt and a couple of battered cars stood abandoned on the edge of the tarmac. A man was trundling a tyre round to the airline which hung in black rubber loops on a rusty wire gate. He glanced at me and said, 'Help you?'

I said, 'Could you tell me where the workshop is, please?'

The man looked me up and down and I wished I had put on something less feminine. I was still wearing the frilled and ruffled clothes I had put on in the morning. He jerked his thumb in the direction of a large building at the back which looked like an old aircraft hanger. 'Over there,' he said.

Trying to look nonchalant, I walked across to it and arrived at a small red-painted metal door over which was a notice saying MIND YOUR HEAD. I banged on it with my knuckles but Radio One was blaring loudly from inside and nobody came. Cautiously, I pushed open the door and went in, ducking my head and stepping over the metal sill. Nick was leaning into the open bonnet of a car and my stomach tightened with the painful clutch of excitement which I always felt when I saw him. A sandy-haired boy in a boiler suit black with grease came up and said, 'Did you want something?'

'Yeah,' I said in my tough voice. 'Want a word with Nick.'

He said, 'Hang on,' and went across to the car. Nick straightened up and looked round, frowning. When he saw me he came across, wiping his hands on an oily rag.

'What you doing here?' he asked as he approached.

'That's a nice greeting,' I said. 'I brought your shirt.' I held up the carrier bag. He didn't look a bit pleased. 'Don't you want to see it?' I asked. And thought, don't you want to see me? I shouldn't have come.

'Not in here,' he said impatiently, indicating his greasy hands. 'I mean, it's great of you to make it, but this isn't the place for a fashion parade, is it?'

'No,' I said. 'Sorry.' I turned to go.

Gary walked past holding a gallon can of oil and said, surprised, 'Hello, Sasha.' He and Nick glanced at each other and I felt even worse.

'Here, wait a minute,' said Nick as I fled towards the door. He caught me up. 'Mind that handle, it's greasy.' He opened the door with the rag in his hand and followed me out. It wasn't so bad in the fresh air. I turned to face him.

'I've got a new job,' I told him, trying to sound business-like. 'Just what I wanted, in the fashion trade.' Perhaps this was the final time I would see him. I gazed at his face as if to grab this last chance of remembering him, the hard lines of his cheeks and chin, the wide mouth and dark-fringed eyes. His nose was smudged with dirt and I felt an impulse to lick my hanky as Mum used to do when I was little, and wipe it off. Then I remembered how much I hated her doing that.

128

'Great,' Nick was saying. 'I didn't think you'd stay to work out the last week at the shoe shop. I could never stay after I'd got the push, not unless they had a week's money in hand. Most of them do.'

I wanted to say something about the party on Sunday, but I couldn't.

'I'll pay you back that tenner tomorrow,' he said. It was better than nothing but I supposed he was just tying up the loose ends. Finishing things off.

'I can't be in the park, I'll be at work,' I said, trying to match his coolness.

'Ron's at six o'clock, then?' he asked. I nodded. He stood and looked at me uncertainly and on an impulse I stood on tiptoe and kissed him. He held his arms out sideways so as not to touch me with his greasy overalls but he kissed me back.

'Now you've got a smut on your nose,' he said. He grinned suddenly. 'Go on, Lolly-top. See you tomorrow.'

I said, 'Great! See you.'

I walked off across the forecourt then turned to wave, but the red-painted door was already closing behind him.

Liz was sitting on the steps behind Mario's, her arms dangling on her white-trousered knees. 'Hello,' she said. 'You look posh. You've got a smut on your nose, though.' I rubbed it with the back of my hand and she said, 'Hang on. I'll get you a bit of paper towel.'

She got up and disappeared into the kitchen then came out with a flapping sheet of soft paper and a dab of butter on her finger. 'Here,' she said, rubbing the butter on my smut then polishing me off as if I was a tureen. 'Engine oil, I suppose.'

I nodded happily and Liz sat down again. 'You are a twit about that bloke,' she said. 'What you been doing, anyway?'

I sat on the step beside her and told her all about it. I told her about Mum, too, and how I had raised her suspicions about Dad without meaning to. Liz shook her head. The highlights made her look as if she'd got mange. 'I don't know,' she said. 'For someone who gets into agonies so easily, you don't half go round sticking your neck out. Still, I'm glad

129

about this job. Sounds great.'

The chef came to the door. 'Your timer's ringing,' he said to Liz. She jumped to her feet with a cry of 'Macaroons!' and ran into the kitchen, reappearing for a moment with her hands in a double-ended oven cloth. 'See you!' she said, and was gone. Work was all very well, I thought gloomily, but it didn't half muck up your social life.

I trailed home again, hoping Mum would not notice that I still carried the shirt in its bag, but as I approached the house I heard the piano, so I knew I was safe. I went upstairs and sat on the windowsill listening to the tinkling music and looking out at the quiet gardens.

Dad was so pleased about the job with the Abrahams that he was bubbling over. He was obviously delighted to have been able to do something for me and his enthusiasm almost won me over. In any case, I knew I must be careful not to do anything to arouse Mum's suspicions any further. The thought of Mum's reaction if she found out was more than I could cope with.

Mr Abraham had rung Dad, true to his promise, confirming that he was willing to take me as an apprentice with a Day Release arrangement so that I could go to art school as well. My course would lead to a City and Guilds qualification. It all sounded wonderful.

I was up early the next morning to be in good time for my new job. I got there well before eight o'clock but the place was already bustling with activity. For quite a while nobody took any notice of me. Bernard was rushing about with swatches of pattern samples and everyone else had jobs to do and was getting on with them. My cheerfulness began to evaporate.

At last a thin woman of about forty came in and said, 'Sasha Bowman?' I got up and said, 'Yes,' and she shook hands formally. 'I am Barbara Golding,' she said. 'I will be looking after you for the first stages of your training.' I noticed that she assumed that I was there permanently although this morning had at first been mentioned as a trial day. It didn't matter. I was sure I would stay. She took me to a corner of a workbench by the window where there was no machine and I wondered what I was going to do.

'Have you got a thimble?' she asked. I shook my head. I had never used a thimble. But then, I didn't use a needle much, either. It was so much quicker to run everything up on the machine. She smiled at my look of dismay. 'When we say start from the bottom,' she said, 'that is exactly what we mean. Hand finishing is important in this trade. You need to be able to sew, even if you don't use it much later on.' And she showed me. Fine, sharp needle, thimble on the third finger, short thread. I asked why it wasn't better to use a long thread so that you didn't have to re-thread the needle so often.

'A long thread will twist,' she told me. 'If you get a knot and have to untangle it, you are wasting precious minutes, and time is your most valuable commodity. Now, let me see you start.'

I thought she was going to slap my wrist when I rolled the thread between finger and thumb and tied a knot in the end. 'Never do that!' she scolded me. 'If you twist your thread of course it will knot. Start with a couple of small back-stitches and leave the end of the thread loose to clip off later.'

I was not allowed to work on a real garment. A derisory pile of fabric off-cuts was good enough for me to practise on. I felt extremely insignificant.

It was a long day. We worked until six and I was terrified that Nick would not wait for me if I was late. I burst breathlessly into Ron's café but he was there, his foot up on the bench seat beside him and his arm dangled across his knee, a roll-up between his fingers. I slid into the seat opposite him and leaned across the table to give him a kiss.

'What you been doing?' he asked. He didn't seem worried that I was late. I explained. 'Sounds hell to me,' he said. 'Why d'you let them piss you about like that? Sew any way you like, can't you?'

A few days ago I would have agreed with him. Even at this moment there was a tiny resentment at the back of my mind at the way I had been regarded as a total beginner with no ability whatever. And yet, perversely, I liked it. I sensed that the job was deliberately made as unattractive and demeaning as possible in order to test the determination of a would-be apprentice. I knew that if I grumbled, I would be out. I could see in my mind's eye Mr Abraham's regretful shake of the head and Bernard's cheerful shrug. 'Take it or leave it, darling,' he would say. It was all up to me.

I tried to explain all this to Nick and he leaned his head back against the seat and blew a smoke ring. 'Up to you, then, innit,' he said, echoing my own thoughts. 'It's your life.' He took a folded ten pound note out of the pocket of his leather jacket and slid it across the table to me. 'Thanks a lot,' he said. He nodded at the carrier bag I had been carting about all day and added, 'That my shirt?'

His hands were fairly clean so I passed the bag over to him. He shook the shirt free of its tissue wrappings and held it up. 'Cor!' he said. 'That's amazing! Aren't you clever!'

'I'm dying to see it on you,' I said.

He took his foot off the bench and got up. Standing in the middle of the café with the shirt in his hand, he trod his cigarette out on the floor then said, 'Hold this a minute.' He threw me the shirt, stripped off his leather jacket and the faded orange tee shirt which he wore under it and, naked to the waist, struck a Mr Universe pose. Several customers clapped and whistled. I handed him the shirt and he put it on, unzipping his jeans to tuck it in.

'There,' he said as he pulled the zip up again. 'How do I look?' He tried to see himself in the mirror behind the counter and Ron moved aside obligingly.

'D'you make that, did you?' a man in a donkey jacket asked me from the next table. I nodded. 'Make one for me?' he asked, grinning.

'Hands off,' said Nick. 'That's my privilege.' He ruffled my hair and bent down to give me a kiss. 'Thanks, Lolly-top,' he said. 'It's great!' He looked at himself again in the mirror, bouffed up an imaginary head of permed hair with his hand and blew a kiss at his ironically-applauding audience. 'Two coffees, two biscuits,' he said to the grinning Ron. '*Please!*'

'There's a good boy,' said Ron.

'Don't know why you're going off to learn dressmaking,' Nick said as he sat down again. He inspected the cuffs and buttons of his shirt, stroking it. 'I reckon you've got it sussed.'

I shook my head. I had learned a lot today. 'The style's okay,' I said, 'but it isn't well made. I used too long a stitch length, to start with, and there's no interfacing in the collar band. I wouldn't dare show it to the Abrahams.' And yet, when Dad had first mentioned them, it had gone through my mind that I might do exactly that.

'Well, it looks all right to me,' he said as Ron brought the coffee. 'Here – how about going to the pictures? There's a good war film on. Something about the SAS, all blood and guts.'

'I'd love to,' I said at once, although I hated blood and guts films. I wished I could say something about Sunday and the dark-haired girl. Didn't I have any pride? But it was Nick who broached the subject.

'You didn't mind about Sunday night, did you?' he asked through a mouthful of biscuit, and went on at once, 'I mean, yes, you mind like hell but – not *really* mind?' He took my hand across the table. I stared into his eyes with the dark-rimmed irises. I didn't mind anything.

'You see,' Nick went on, 'It might have been you. At a party, people get a bit pissed, they'll do anything. And it wouldn't have been fair. You haven't decided about all that, and the pill and everything. I shouldn't have done it, I know. I'm really sorry about it. I just went off to look up a few friends and there she was.'

'I suppose you've known her for ages,' I said lightly.

'She's the rich one I told you about,' said Nick. 'Daddy with the Porsche.' He shrugged. 'It's nothing to her,' he said. 'Just another little amusement. Cars, parties, blokes. But at least I know there'll be no come-back. Nobody gets hurt.' Then he put his hand over mine. 'You're different,' he said. 'You really mean it. That makes you a lot more hurtable.'

Although I treasured what he said, I laughed. How ironic.

133

Was that life's golden rule? Only make love when you are not in love? The big moment would only be mine when I no longer cared whether it happened or not.

Nick was looking at me with some concern. 'Are you all right?' he asked.

I managed not to sigh. 'Yes,' I said. 'I'm all right.'

When we had finished our coffee I rang Mum to say I was going out. She *did* sigh. 'You always seem to choose a night when your father is out,' she said. So he was seeing the woman again. The bastard. 'Look,' I said, 'I'll come home. I'm sorry, I didn't know he was out.'

'Don't be silly,' she said crossly. 'If you've made your arrangements you must stick to them. I'll be all right. Just you go and enjoy yourself.'

'Are you sure?' I persisted. But I didn't want to go home. I wanted to go to the pictures with Nick. Mum's presence through the telephone was tense, resentful. She hadn't answered my polite question and she hadn't rung off. 'Well – see you later, then,' I said lamely, and hung up.

We had sausages and tomatoes and chips at Ron's and then went down the High Street to the cinema. Years ago it had been huge but now it was divided into three small viewing theatres. Ours was Studio Two. Violence raged on the screen and Nick had his arm round me, kissing me in the intervals between the high spots of the film's beastliness. I began to ache because of sitting sideways in my seat but I didn't want him to think I was moving away, so I went on aching. A man shot another man – I had lost track of the plot – and his face exploded into a mess of blood. I tried to remember that it was only a film, just trick photography, but it was horrible. I shut my eyes when the next gun was aimed. 'Cor, look at that,' said Nick. I hid my face against his leather jacket and his fingers groped for the buttons of my blouse. The velour of the seat prickled the underside of my thighs through my cotton skirt. There in the dark it felt like privacy, though we had never been alone in a room together.

Afterwards, we went for a drink before the pubs closed then walked slowly back to my house. I didn't have my crash-helmet with me and in any case it was near enough not to need the bike.

In the lamp-lit street, I thought that things were all right again. There had been a kind of explanation about Sunday, even a kind of apology. And he had almost said he cared. I accepted his detachment and he tolerated my love. It wasn't a happy arrangement but I would rather be unhappy with him than without him. In our odd way, we understood each other.

'What are you doing at the weekend?' I asked. 'I get Saturdays off at this place.'

'Working in the morning,' he said. 'Then I better stay in because of the bike. Didn't tell you, did I? I finished the Triumph. Got an advert coming out in tomorrow's paper.'

'Oh, good,' I said.

'Had to give my mate's address,' he went on. 'Can't have it at the flat. So I'll be round there all day.' He had never told me his mate's address, or even his name. Obviously he thought it simply didn't concern me. 'Got to chat up the punters, you see,' he added. 'Never get your price otherwise.'

'What about the evening?' I ventured. 'If you've sold the bike, I mean.' And I knew at once I should not have asked. He did not answer for a minute. We reached the gate of my house and stopped under the laburnum tree. I could hear Mum playing the piano.

He turned me to face him. 'Look,' he said, 'you never get the message, do you? Don't keep pushing it. You're all right – I like you a lot. But we've got to be free, haven't we? I don't own you. You don't own me. So let's leave it like that. Okay?'

'If that's the way you want it,' I said bravely. 'It's all right by me.' But I was beginning to shake. 'Anything you do is all right by me,' I told him angrily. 'Just anything. That's the whole trouble.' And I broke away from him and ran into the house, and up the stairs to my bedroom. I didn't put the light on. Through my tears I looked out of the window, down to where the street lamp flickered through the laburnum leaves. A small flame shone into his face as he bent his head to light a cigarette from the match in his cupped hands. Then he flicked the match into the gutter and walked away.

135

Chapter 12

I didn't want to get up the next morning. It was a Saturday and there was nothing to look forward to. Dad had been out again last night, unwittingly rubbing it in that he had a girl friend with dark hair and smooth bare arms. I saw her face again in my mind's eye, smiling up at him as she turned to slip on the coat he held for her. I did not want to think about it but it was impossible to forget.

And Nick. Since he had made himself so clear last night, there was no point in deluding myself any more. It was all over. Nothing remained now except to find a way to stop caring.

It wasn't Nick's fault that he didn't love me, I argued with myself. He didn't mean to be cruel. He was trying hard to avoid that very thing. I had ruined it through my own clumsy fault, making him feel trapped. Love to me meant sharing my whole existence – my feelings, my abilities, my possessions, everything – with no reserve whatever. It was something very different to him. He seemed almost to fear it. His mother had left home. She could not have been loved, or why would she have gone? His father was a hot-tempered, violent man. Perhaps Nick for all his outward confidence, feared the effects of strong emotion. Perhaps someone patient enough and loving enough would at last kindle some trust in him, like a wild pony slowly learning confidence. But was I that person?

I stared at the ceiling where a few flies circled in the morning sun. Each time they nearly met they accelerated away on a new elliptical path, only to return. I ought to give him up, I thought. Stop thinking about him. Bring my mind back into my own self like a snail retracting its horns. But it felt like death.

The telephone rang. I heard my mother answer it, then she

came running upstairs and tapped at my door. 'It's Bernard Abraham,' she said. 'He wants to talk to you.'

I jumped up and grabbed my kimono.

'Listen, darling.' His fat, sketchy voice radiated energy. 'What you doing this afternoon?'

'Nothing,' I said.

'Good. You know Michael Bancroft? No? Doesn't matter. He's the best photographer there is. Marvellous guy, you should see his pictures. What am I saying? You will, you will. Listen, can you get here this afternoon? We want to do pictures for my catalogue.'

'What time?' I asked, trying to sound as if this sort of thing happened to me every day.

'Half-past two,' said Bernard. 'No, he won't be here so early. Three o'clock. Okay, darling? At the workroom.'

'Three o'clock,' I said, and he rang off.

I went and had a bath and washed my hair. I topped up the mauvy-pink dye and did it up in pipe cleaners then went downstairs to get some coffee. My father was in the kitchen reading the paper. Mum called through from the utility room where she was unloading the washing machine, 'David, you really must do something about that tree stump.'

'M'm,' he said, still reading.

'That old sycamore by the shed,' she persisted. 'It's no good cutting trees down if you don't put some creosote on them to kill the roots. It's been putting out new shoots all summer and I've kept cutting them off. Now, don't forget!'

'Right!' he called cheerfully, not raising his eyes from the newspaper. When she had gone out he glanced at me with a look of complicity which I would usually have responded to and said, 'I knew I'd get it in the neck about that.'

I didn't answer. Don't you appeal to me for sympathy, I thought angrily. I could never take his part against Mum again. Not now. I turned away to the fridge for a bottle of milk. Then, suddenly afraid he was going to challenge me about my curtness, I said, 'I'm going to model for some fashion photographs this afternoon, for Bernard Abraham.'

'Are you, love?' He put his paper down with real interest.

He laughed. 'Joss said Bernard was tickled to death with your hair. I think you'll be just what they need, you know. Someone to put them in touch with all this teenage culture people talk about. Are you getting on well with them?'

'Yes, I think so,' I said stiffly. 'Bernard's a bit of a sharp businessman but Mr Abraham is very nice. And so is his wife.'

'Myra.' My father gave a reminiscent smile. 'You should have seen that girl when Joss first met her. Skin and bone. She was a survivor of Belsen, you know. Lost all her family and spent months in a reception camp then somehow made her way to England. I don't know the full story. She doesn't talk about it.'

'Oh, *no*!' I couldn't believe it. Little dark-eyed Myra, a part of the horror I had seen on the grainy news-reel photographs? Bulldozers, corpses, gas-chambers? I felt sick.

'Oh, yes,' said my father grimly.

Mum came to the back door. 'Look, what *about* this tree stump?' she demanded. My father put his paper on the table and got up. 'See you later,' he said to me, as though there was more to tell me. I took my cup of coffee and went slowly upstairs.

'Great!' said Bernard when I arrived at the workroom. 'You look marvellous!' I didn't feel marvellous despite all my efforts with make-up and hair. I could not stop my mind from running in crazy circles on the nagging, painful topics of Nick and my father. They seemed to collide and veer apart like the flies circling under my bedroom ceiling. I wanted to talk to my father about the Abrahams and about what he had told me but I was stifled with rage at his duplicity. I wanted to talk to Nick about my father but Nick was not there. I would never talk to him about anything. I thought of a man I had overheard in Ron's referring to his wife as 'my other half'. He had used the phrase ironically but there had been some reason for it to come into the English language, I thought. People needed their other halves. At least, I did. I kept wanting to cry.

Bernard led the way into the workroom where the benches

had been moved to make a space. A neat, grey-haired man was standing on one of them, adjusting a spotlight on a stand.

'Here's the beautiful girl,' announced Bernard with his hand on my back. 'Sasha Bowman. Sasha, this is Michael Bancroft.'

Michael nodded and said, 'Hello.' Then he stared at me in an objective kind of way and added, 'Nice. Very zappy. You done any modelling before, dear?'

'No,' I said. I tried to smile at him.

'Never mind,' said Michael. 'You'll soon pick it up. Better make a start, Bernie.'

'Right,' said Bernard. 'Come on, darling, you can change in the office.' The office wasn't very private, I thought, with its glass walls looking on to the workroom. But I realised that neither Bernard nor Michael thought of me as an individual girl. For their purposes, I was the means of displaying the dresses.

'Jersey dress with a drawstring waist,' said Bernard, taking it off the rail and slipping the hanger out of it. 'You want a hand?'

'No, thanks,' I said. The dress was peacock blue, a colour I hated.

He nodded. 'Some do, some don't,' he said. 'Come out when you're ready.'

They both looked at me critically when I went out.

'Bit baggy,' said Michael.

'No problem,' said Bernard. 'Turn round, darling.' He took great handfuls of the dress down my back and pinned it firmly so that the bodice looked figure-hugging. I felt as if I had been sewn into it.

'Better,' said Michael. 'We'll try it like that.'

Lights blazed from all directions. 'What shall I do?' I asked nervously.

'Move about,' said Michael. 'Sit on that tall chair, foot on the rail, foot off, lean against it, smile up, smile round, smile at me – there's a kind of rhythm to it. Look.' He went into a pantomime which would have made me giggle if it wasn't for the sadness and the weird feeling that this wasn't real.

'Give it a try,' said Michael, retreating behind the terrifying little eye of his camera on its long tripod. He didn't seem to like me very much.

I gave it a try. I felt stiff and silly.

'Don't you ever smile, dear?' said Michael, who had not taken a single picture. 'You look like you're going to a funeral. Come on, now, zip-zip-zip! Glorious day, top of the world – give us a bit of animation. Where's that tape, Bern?'

They turned on some pop music. It helped a bit, but not much. I smiled dementedly at the wall and the ceiling and wherever I was told. Bernard groaned. 'What's the matter with you?' he asked. 'Talk about the clown with the broken heart! You're not the girl you were yesterday, darling – what's wrong with your life?'

I shook my head blindly. 'Nothing,' I muttered. I had been so stupid to think I could do this.

The door opened and Mr and Mrs Abraham came in. Myra was carrying a big basket over her arm and she went over to Bernard and kissed him, smiling at me at the same time. She was obviously very proud of her big son. I thought of Belsen.

Mr Abraham gave me a hug. 'How's it going, Sasha?' he asked. Michael and Bernard glanced at each other and I said, 'It's terrible.'

'It's a very difficult thing to do,' said Mr Abraham seriously. 'It's not natural to be natural, you see. Not when you're aware of it.'

I took a very deep breath and determined that I would make a success of this. I *mustn't* let them down. Or myself, either.

'Big smile,' said Michael, switching on the lights and the tape recorder. As I moved the camera clicked at what seemed to me to be a breakneck speed. Why was he taking so *many* photographs?

'Right,' he said at last. 'Try the next one.'

'Jumpsuit,' said Bernard. 'Mother, will you unpin her?'

Myra followed me into the office. Her grasp was as firm and business-like as Bernard's as she whipped the pins out of the jersey dress, slid the zip down and slipped it off my shoulders.

'Step out of it,' she advised. 'Then you won't mess up your hair or your make-up.' She helped me into a jumpsuit in bright yellow cotton with blue and red stripes across the chest and arms. 'In this you have to look happy,' she said gravely. 'Yes?'

I nodded. And in the next instant I was in floods of tears.

'Oh, there, there,' she said. 'Sit down, my darling. Don't get mascara on the jumpsuit. What is it?' She produced a box of tissues from somewhere and pulled them out one after another in such quantities that I would have laughed if I hadn't been crying so much. The awful thing was, I knew everyone outside could see me. Myra sat down beside me and put her arm round my shoulders. She was so much smaller than me that I felt huge and stupid.

'Tell me what's the matter,' she said. She sounded as if she was really concerned. 'It's not just the photographs, is it?' she went on. 'Something else. It's a boy friend. It's your family.' She was not going to take no for an answer. I nodded. 'Which is it?' she asked sympathetically.

'Both,' I wailed, and gave a gulping laugh because it sounded so silly.

'Boy friends – that I can understand,' she said. 'Love is a terrible thing. It's like an illness. You catch it, and there's nothing you can do until it's better. Sometimes you recover. Sometimes you carry the scars. But scars don't hurt.'

I looked at her wrinkled face with its pointed chin and dark-fringed eyes and thought of the things she must have seen. If anyone carried scars, she did.

'What else?' she asked insistently. 'Some trouble with your father?'

I nodded again, in a fresh flood of tears, and Mr Abraham came in. He seemed quite unsurprised to see me crying, though he said, 'Oh, dear, dear,' in a concerned sort of way.

'Joss,' said Myra, 'Sasha is upset about her father.'

'Yes,' he said thoughtfully. 'You gave me that impression on Thursday, Sasha. What's he been up to?'

'He's been seeing another woman,' I blurted out.

Now that I had said it, I wondered why it had seemed so

dreadful. The Abrahams looked at each other and Joss nodded. 'Have you told him you know?' he asked.

'I can't,' I said in utter despondency. 'I just can't talk to him. And I want to.' This seemed to be the dead centre of all the awfulness.

'Well,' said Mr Abraham, sitting down with Myra and me, 'you can talk to us. You won't think we are interfering? If we are to know each other and work together, troubles like this are best shared, I think.' I nodded. 'Then let me tell you,' he went on. 'First of all, your father thinks the world of you. We know each other very well, David and I, and every time we meet it is Susan this, Susan that. Or Sasha, now that you've changed your name.'

For the first time, I almost wished I had stuck to the name I had been given. Perhaps it had been hurtful of me to reject it. But Joss was going on, 'And the next thing is, yes, you are quite right. He has this friend. Did you see them together?'

I nodded. 'In a restaurant,' I said. 'She's got dark hair. Slim. About forty – perhaps more.'

'Her name is Laura Sheridan,' he said. 'Her husband was killed in an accident last year, driving a car while drunk. It was not an unusual thing for him to do, unfortunately. Laura's life with him was not a happy one. She and your father had known each other for a long, long time. Many years.'

'I don't understand,' I said. 'That doesn't make it any better, just because they've been having this affair for ages.'

He took my hand. 'Listen,' he said, 'you understand about love. It's not a thing you switch on and off.'

Myra laughed. 'I've just been telling her it's a disease,' she said.

I saw that Bernard had come to stand in the doorway. Oh, great, I thought bitterly. Let's all join the party. 'Gotta be love,' Bernard said. 'Mother's always on about it's a disease. Before I got married, such a time I had! He rolled his eyes. 'Every new girl friend, a new family crisis. Listen, Michael wants to be off by six, okay?' He, too, seemed quite unruffled by my collapse. Perhaps they were used to people behaving this way. He smiled at me kindly, his fat face creasing. 'When you're ready, darling. Take your time. Get your face together.' He went out again.

'Never mind about him,' said Myra. 'Listen to what I'm telling you. When you fall in love, you feel as if nobody else has ever suffered this way. It seems to be something overwhelming – too strong to stand up to.' I nodded agreement. 'Then you understand about your father and Laura,' said Myra simply.

'Not Dad,' I said. 'He can't. He's older. He's married.'

The Abrahams shook their heads. 'It's exactly the same,' said Myra. 'It's almost impossible to stop loving. Specially when there seems no good reason.'

'I know,' I said bleakly. 'But if he loves this Laura Sheridan, why didn't he marry her instead of Mum?'

There was a pause. For the first time, I sensed that there was something the Abrahams didn't want to tell me. Then Joss said, 'There *was* a good reason.'

And then I understood. 'You mean,' I said, 'he married Mum because she was pregnant? With me?'

They looked at each other uneasily. 'My dear, it happens to so many people,' said Myra. 'And there are worse reasons for a marriage. Both of them wanted you, you see. Both of them loved you.'

'I know,' I said. It explained so much. Poor Dad. And poor Mum as well. It was all so sad. And then I realised something else. 'If he loved Laura first,' I said, 'before he knew Mum – but he had to marry Mum . . .' I wished I had not started to say it: 'Then he was being unfaithful to Laura all that time, wasn't he?' I ended unhappily. And my mind jumped back to the party, when Nick and the dark-haired girl had come out of that room, smiling at each other. Did loving someone *always* have to hurt?

'There is no such thing as perfection,' Myra said gently. 'Everyone does the best they can. We are all held together by a kind of love. The reasons for the way we behave always seem good at the time. It's only afterwards we look back and wonder why.'

Bernard glanced in through the glass. This was no time to

think about what Myra had told me. I said, 'What am I going to do about my face?'

'Wash it,' said Myra promptly. 'Then put on heaps of make-up and laugh a lot and you will look fine.'

And I did.

'Terrific!' said Michael. 'Marvellous! Go–go–go!' He kept up a stream of meaningless good cheer while I cavorted about in the yellow jumpsuit like a kid on a beach. The relief of having talked to somebody was so terrific that I felt charged with a kind of mad energy. The pace quickened and I rushed in and out of the office to tear off one garment and put on another, with Myra doing up zips, snatching up clothes from where I dropped them to replace them on hangers, pushing my hair into order and insistently powdering my face from an ancient-looking box of Leichner theatrical make-up. 'I don't care what these modern people say,' she declared. 'Shiny noses are not pretty.'

'Sing!' commanded Michael, and I did. 'Dance!' he said madly, 'grab the sun from the sky! Lovely! Lovely!'

At last it was over. Michael switched the lights out for the last time and I slumped in the office in my bra and pants, suddenly too exhausted to face the task of putting my own clothes on again. Myra had disappeared but in a few minutes she came back with a tray of coffee and chocolate cake. Briskly, she held out my shirt and I put it on then climbed into my jeans.

Bernard came in and pushed twenty pounds into my hand. 'You're great, darling,' he said. 'This is just for starters. You'll be worth lots more if you keep it up.'

'Don't go into the model business,' advised Myra, handing me a cup of coffee. 'Good money, yes, but it's a short life and what have you got at the end? Nothing.'

'In any case,' I said, 'I want to be a designer.'

When Michael had packed up all his stuff, it was getting dark outside and Myra said, 'Everyone come and have some supper, yes? Bernard, will you pick up Leila from home?'

Bernard shook his head. 'We're going to the Jacobsons,' he said. He glanced at his watch and added, 'Is that the time?

She'll murder me.'

'Then you'll come, Sasha,' said Myra. 'Michael, do you really have to go somewhere else?'

''Fraid so,' said Michael. 'Posh do tonight. Photos for *Harpers*.'

So I rang up home once again to say I would be late. This time it was Dad who answered. When I had explained what I was doing and he had said it was fine there was a pause. I wanted to say something to him but I didn't know what. At last I said, 'Did you do the tree stump?'

I heard his dry chuckle. 'Yes,' he said. 'Put paid to that. Thanks for ringing, love.' And the silence still clung between us.

'It's all right,' I said, and wished I could think of something else. ''Bye.'

I had assumed that the Abrahams lived over the shop in Peckham but we went to a big mansion flat in Finchley Road. It was furnished in a heavy, old-fashioned way with lots of velvet and mahogany, and there was none of the clutter which characterised the little room in Peckham. Myra made a chicken *pilau* and we talked for a long time about the fashion trade and modern designers, and there was no reference made to anything personal. It was as though that subject had been dealt with quite fully enough and there was no point in saying anything more about it. I was glad, for I was beginning to feel that they might regard me as a 'problem', which would have been awful. As it was, they were very funny with their anecdotes about temperamental models and famous women who refused to accept that they were getting fat, and I thoroughly enjoyed the evening.

When I got up to go they both kissed me and it seemed natural to embrace them although I would not have dreamed of hugging most of the people I knew, except for my father. And Nick. I laughed and said, 'It's nice, all this kissing and hugging!'

Myra said, 'Of course it's nice. I can't stand the stiff English, never touch each other!' I thought of my mother,

145

locked in her resentful solitude. She never touched anyone. Myra added, 'Listen, Sasha, don't keep troubles to yourself. The more you think about them the more they grow. You can always come and talk to Joss or me. If you want to, that is.'

Joss said, 'The main thing is to be able to work. Nobody is without troubles but they are not disasters unless they stop you working.'

I thought it sounded a pretty dismal idea but Myra nodded agreement. 'He is right,' she said. 'You will see.'

I thought about it all the way home on the Underground. In a way, I did understand what Joss meant, but it all depended on what sort of work you were doing. At the shoe shop I had just worked for money, wishing the time away, measuring the effort I put in against the reward at the end of the week. But when I was trying to draw something or work out an idea for a design, I was completely occupied in an effort that was more important to me than anything else. It was such a funny thing to try and explain, even to myself. It was as though a part of the essential me was struggling to find existence in the form of a thing which could be seen and have its own being. That kind of work had nothing to do with earning money. If money resulted from doing it, so much the better, for it would release me from the necessity of working at something else simply in order to live. But the work I wanted to do was based on a compulsive fascination. Even Nick could not extinguish that. But, looking back, I had to admit that my anguish over him in the last few weeks had meant that very little drawing had been done, and most of it had consisted of interminable unsuccessful sketches of Nick, whose true appearance always eluded me.

I got out at my station and went up the escalator and out into the familiar High Street. I glanced in at the lit windows of the shoe shop where I had worked, noticing with amusement that Mrs Marshall had put a display of school shoes in place of the beach sandals. Thank Heavens I wasn't there to cram the reluctant little feet with their energetically mobile toes into the stiff brown lace-ups. Children always hated school shoes.

The Plumbers Arms was ahead of me and I thought with nostalgia of the first time I had been in there with Nick on the evening we came back from Westerham. I remembered how cold I had felt with my bare arms and legs, but how hot the day had been. It was dark earlier now, and the mornings were sharp and dewy.

The brightly-lit door of the saloon bar opened and a girl came out. With a start of pleasure, I saw that it was Liz. I almost called to her but then I realised that the boy who came through the door behind her was not Gary but Nick.

They started along the pavement in front of me, and I saw Nick put his arm round Liz's shoulders casually. I could feel the weight of that arm, smell the closeness of the leather jacket. I ducked into a shop doorway, terrified that they would look back for some reason and see me, though I thought bitterly that there was no reason why *I* should feel guilty.

I stood staring senselessly at piles of flanelette sheets and some garments called Plated Vests, and fury grew in me. Just wait until I saw Liz. I nursed my anger as a defence against misery. My face was red with it, my fists clenched. I looked out of the shop doorway cautiously. There was no sign of Nick and Liz.

At least my crash-helmet was in my bedroom at home, I thought with bitter satisfaction. He couldn't give it to her and go off somewhere with her on the bike. Then I thought, he only lent it to me. Perhaps it goes the rounds, being used for each current girl friend as she comes along. Others wore it before me. And now Liz would want it. I must give the beastly thing back, I thought savagely, and then they could get on with it.

I went home. My parents sat watching the television in the sitting-room and I thought when I came into the room they would know from my face that something terrible had happened but they just glanced up casually and asked how I had got on and whether I wanted some tea. I sat down with them and talked about the photographic session and drank a cup of tea and the normality of it all seemed like a dream. All the time in my mind I was conducting a furious row with Liz, who had called herself a friend. When I had finished my tea I got up and said, 'Must just ring Liz.' It could not wait until the morning.

'At this hour?' Mum protested. I took no notice. Apart from anything else, I wanted to know whether Liz was home yet. If she was not, then she had even more to answer for. I dialled her number and waited. It rang for a long time. At last her mother answered. 'Yes?' she said.

I asked boldly, 'Is Liz there?'

'No, she bloody isn't,' she snapped. 'And I don't know what you think you're doing getting me out of bed at bloody midnight. Why can't you kids think of other people?' And she slammed the phone down.

My blood was up. If they weren't at Liz's, perhaps he had taken her back to the flat. Treat him rough, she had advised me. Right, then. With no idea of what I was going to say, I dialled Nick's number.

This time it rang even longer. Then a cross voice said, 'What is it?'

I gulped. I had forgotten about Nick's father. 'I'm sorry to disturb you,' I said politely, 'but I was trying to find a friend of mine called Liz.'

'Oh, were you?' he snarled. 'Well, you want your flaming head read. Nick!' he bellowed. '*Nick!* One of your bloody women on the phone. *Nick!*' His voice sounded more distant as it called again. Then it said in my ear, 'He's out. Now, piss off.' And he, too, hung up.

Rather shakily, I replaced the receiver. When I went back into the sitting-room, transmission had finished and Dad was getting up to switch off the television. I wondered why I wasn't in floods of tears. I seemed to be watching myself as if I was a puppet operated in some remote way by my own control. Mum was looking reproachful. 'You really shouldn't ring people up at this time of night, dear,' she said. 'I'd be frightfully cross if anyone did it to me.'

Join the club, I thought drearily. Aloud, I said, 'Yes. I expect you would.'

Chapter 13

I didn't try to ring Liz up the next morning. If her mother answered, I would get another telling off about ringing so late last night, for I was sure she had recognised my voice. And anyway, what was the use? I didn't know what to say. The fury of last night had left me and I ached with depression.

I went down in my kimono for some coffee and took it upstairs. After I had drunk it I put on a pair of jeans and an old shirt and tried to settle down to some designs. I had been thinking about an evening coat in dark green velvet bound with self-coloured satin but it was something I could never make because it would be far too expensive. This morning I could not even find it interesting. By Mr Abraham's definition, my troubles really were a disaster.

I looked out into the garden. My father was inspecting the stump of the sycamore tree. I could see the holes he had drilled in it and the dark blots of creosote spilling across the creamy wood. The shoots which surrounded it were already beginning to droop and I felt sad about the death which had been sown in the tree. The beginning of the end, I thought.

The morning wore on and the smell of roasting meat began to drift up from the kitchen. I decided that Liz was not going to turn up. If she didn't, it would be the first Sunday for nearly a year that we had not met. Just as well, I thought grimly. It would leave a lot of hurtful things unsaid. But I felt miserable that she wouldn't come and face me. It was such an underhand way for a friendship to end. I sat on my bed with my hands between my knees. Everything hurt, not just as a physical pain but as a bruising of the senses. The squares of sunlight on the wall, each tuft of the pink carpet, the very air which filled the quiet room; it all hurt.

I took 'Goodbye, Summer' from half way down the pile of

records, for I had not played it for some time. I wound up the gramophone and put the record on and the clear, far-off voice began its song. I sat on the window sill and listened to its sadness as if I heard it for the first time. Despite the sunshine, I felt cold.

The record was almost over when I heard Liz running up the stairs. She came in, tapping on the door as she opened it, and said breezily, 'Hello! Coo, what a night. Didn't get to bed until four.' She shut the door and leaned back against it as she saw my face. She was wearing her black velvet smoking jacket. The record played on in the silence. All our tomorrows shall be as today.

I said, 'I don't want to hear about it.'

Liz frowned. 'What do you mean?' she asked. And her face turned pink.

'I mean I saw you and Nick coming out of the Plumbers Arms last night,' I said. 'I was walking home from the Underground station. I suppose you thought I was safely parked in front of the telly.' It didn't sound tragic. It sounded abominably crude.

Liz said angrily, 'Look, it wasn't like that! I don't want your precious Nick! He just – '

'Not much you don't!' I shouted. 'Only until four in the morning! I suppose now you're on the pill you can have any bloke you like!'

The record ended and Liz turned sharply to put the playing arm back in its clip. As she picked the record up she glared at me over her shoulder and said furiously, 'Oh, why don't you *grow up*?' And, because she was not looking at what she was doing, the rolled-up sleeve of her smoking jacket caught the raised lid of the gramophone and jerked it free of its supporting bracket. It crashed down across the record and smashed it into several pieces. Liz still held half of it between her finger and thumb. She clapped her other hand to her mouth and tears sprang to her eyes. 'Oh, Sasha,' she said. 'I'm so sorry.'

I stared at it. 'So that really is goodbye,' I said. 'Goodbye to Nick. Goodbye to you. Goodbye, summer.' I did not want to cry but the tears came. I wished it was Myra in the room with me because we would have hugged each other and shared the grief. And yet I knew that Liz did share it, in her way, as we had shared so much.

She fetched the box of Kleenex and put it on the window sill between us, then pulled out a tissue and blew her nose.

'Look,' she said. 'You've got to understand about this. It's not the way you think.' Her blotched eyes stared at me earnestly. 'Some of us went round to the pub after work. We often do on a Saturday night. And Nick was in there with a bloke who had something to do with a bike he'd just sold.'

'The Triumph,' I said dully. It didn't matter any more.

Liz nodded. 'That's what he said,' she agreed. 'Anyway, this bloke had a girl with him and Nick didn't, so he started talking to me.'

I said, 'I don't want to know.'

'Yes, you do,' Liz said firmly. 'Just listen, will you? Nick wanted to talk about you. He was worried about you taking things so seriously. He said he'd thought at first that you were a tough cookie who knew how to take care of herself but he could see now that you were getting upset and he felt bad about it.'

I said, 'Huh!' But Liz went on, 'He said he was thinking of going in the Merchant Navy so it wasn't fair to get involved with anyone. But he does care about you, Sasha. He said he wished he didn't. But he does.'

'Oh, great!' I said. 'So when you'd finished having a heart-to-heart about me you took him to bed for the rest of the night, did you?'

'No, I *didn't*,' said Liz, trying not to get cross. 'He said he wanted to see Gary to pay him back some money he owed him now he'd sold the bike. So I said I was going round to Gary's and he might as well come along, too. I mean – actually, I've more or less moved in with Gary.'

I said, 'Have you?' and she nodded. Then she went on, 'Anyway, Nick bought a half-bottle of gin and put it in his pocket and we went round to Gary's. And what with the gin and playing records and talking about bikes and things, it was four o'clock before Nick went home. I stayed at Gary's. And that's all,' she ended.

I thought about it. 'He had his arm round you,' I said.

'Yes, he did,' Liz agreed. 'He's the kind of bloke who puts his arm round anyone. For God's sake, Sasha, don't be so prudish.'

After a bit I said, 'I am sorry, Liz. Stupid to get it all wrong like that. But you can see how it looked. Specially after the girl at the party.'

'Of course I can,' she agreed. 'I'd have jumped to exactly the same conclusion. I'm sorry, too. I didn't mean to upset you, honest. And I'm terribly sorry about the record.'

I went across to the gramophone and raised the lid.

There it lay, not music any more but bits of smashed black mica. 'It had to end some time,' I said. 'And today seems fitting, somehow. Better than just wearing out.' I started to gather up the pieces.

Liz watched me. 'Sasha,' she said, 'what are you going to do about Nick?'

I dropped the remains of the record into the waste paper basket and stood looking down at them. 'I'm going to try and get over it,' I said.

'Not see him any more?' asked Liz. I nodded. I couldn't say anything. I moved away from the waste paper basket and looked out of the window instead. It didn't make a lot of difference what I looked at, everything still hurt just the same. The green shoots round the sycamore stump seemed to droop a little more. I must stop this sentimental symbolism, I told myself.

'Perhaps it's the best thing,' said Liz 'In a year or two, you never know. It might work marvellously. He does care about you, in his nutty way.'

'I don't think he does,' I said. I thought about it then added, 'I almost hope he doesn't. I don't think I'm strong enough to stop it all by myself. If he keeps coming round, I'll keep seeing him. I know it's stupid. I'm free to choose what I do and who I see – but it doesn't feel like that. We've got to live, haven't we? And living includes Nick. Or it does for me, anyway. But I don't think he'll come here again. He's stronger than me. And he doesn't care as much, so it isn't as hard. He's chosen for me. And the answer's no.'

'Wait and see,' said Liz. 'You may be surprised.' Then she said, 'Gary and I are going to Sweden next week. Off on Sunday.'

'And I'll be going to Aldeburgh,' I said. 'I'll have to tell the Abrahams.'

Liz nodded, and we were quiet. In the ordinary way I would have been in the middle of a highly coloured account of yesterday's photographic session but this morning things like that didn't seem worth the effort of talking about.

'You'll have to sort things out with your dad,' said Liz after a bit, 'or it'll be pretty dreadful in Aldeburgh.'

'I know,' I said. My thoughts about Dad had taken a new shift since talking to the Abrahams yesterday.

'Funny thing,' I said, still looking out of the window, 'but I found out why Mum and Dad got married. The Abrahams sort of let it slip.'

'Go on?' said Liz.

'It was because of me,' I said. 'Shotgun job. It's a laugh, isn't it, after all that respectability?'

Liz didn't laugh. 'Join the club, mate,' she said practically. Then she added, 'But at least you've *had* a father all this time.'

'Yes,' I said. 'Poor old Dad.' I turned from the window to look at Liz and suddenly we grinned at each other. Join the club. Great.

'Look,' said Liz, 'I've got ever so much to do, going away next week. I must try and sort out what I'm going to pack.'

I nodded.

She put her hand on my sleeve. 'Are you all right?' she asked.

'Yes,' I said. 'I'm all right. Like you said, it's time I grew up.'

'Oh, come off it,' Liz protested. 'You know I didn't mean it. I'm going home to sort my things out, okay? I'll see you before I go. I've got a free day on Tuesday.'

'I don't get off until six,' I said.

'We'll go and do something on Tuesday night, then,' she said, and I asked, 'What about Gary?'

'Good Lord,' said Liz impatiently, 'I don't see Gary *all* the time. He's very sweet but there's other things in life as well as him.'

I thought, then you don't feel about Gary the way I feel about Nick. Felt about Nick. Oh, God.

'I'll be off, then,' said Liz. She gave me her uneven grin and added, 'See you Tuesday.'

'Great,' I said. And suddenly our old friendship was there, unchanged. I gave a kind of laugh and said, 'You'd better come round here, you old baggage, or I'll never know where to find you.'

'Okay,' she said, restored to her usual good humour. 'See you.' Then she was clattering down the stairs and I heard the front door slam.

The crash-helmet lay on my dressing-table, looking as outlandish as a space craft among my make-up things. To-morrow I would take it to work and drop in at Ron's for one last time on the way home. But he might be doing overtime. Perhaps it would be better to leave it here. I could come home first and pick it up, then go to Ron's later. Or perhaps I would ring Nick up and tell him to come and collect it. The sooner it was gone the better. It was more merciful to die quickly.

Mum's raised voice sounded from the kitchen and I guessed that Dad had announced his intention of going out for a lunch-time pint. He always suggested that she should go with him but inevitably she launched into a stream of protest about making gravy and the horrors of overcooked cabbage. She was so silly. Why didn't she cook in the evening? Poor Mum.

Impulsively I ran through to my parents' bedroom in the front of the house and looked out. Dad was just latching the gate behind him, very carefully as if to avoid giving any further offence. Then he started off down the road. I ran downstairs and out of the front door, left the gate swinging and caught up with him before he reached the corner.

He stopped. 'Hello, love!' he said. He looked questioning, as though assuming that I had been sent after him with a message.

'Can I come with you?' I asked breathlessly.

His anxiety gave way to surprised relief. 'I'm honoured!' he said with his short laugh, and offered me his arm with the same courtesy I had seen him extend to Laura Sheridan. I couldn't find anything else to say as we walked to the pub. I was beginning to wish I had stayed up in my room. What was I going to say to him? What did I really mean? I hadn't stopped to work it out.

'How's that strapping great Hell's Angel of yours?' he enquired. I suppose he didn't know what to say, either, but he picked the wrong question when he asked that. When I didn't answer he turned his head to look at me then hugged my arm closer to his side. 'You'd think I'd have learned after all these years,' he said, 'not to ask damn' silly questions. I'm sorry, my love. But if it's any consolation, it happens to all of us.'

I could have asked him what he meant, but the fact that I knew prevented it. We walked on in silence until we reached the George. Dad never went to the Plumbers Arms and the George was a gabled, mock-Tudor affair standing behind a car park with a plane tree growing in it.

'Shall we sit in the garden?' Dad suggested. 'It's one of the last sunny days we'll get, I suppose. What would you like to drink?'

I said, 'Just a shandy, please.' I wondered if he didn't want to be seen taking an under-age drinker into the bar and smiled privately because most people thought I was at least twenty. But I didn't argue. I said, 'I'll find a table.'

I went through a brick arch to the garden where a couple of families with young children sat at white-painted metal tables drinking beer in the half-hearted sunshine. A wind had sprung up, blowing puffy clouds across the sky. A toddler sitting on the grass tipped his packet of crisps upside down and shook it vigorously to make sure that every single crisp fell out. Pink and purple asters grew in the border by the fence. I chose a table as far as possible from the families and their children and brushed the leaves off the white-painted surface. Dad came out with my shandy and a pint of bitter for himself and sat down rather cautiously on the slatted chair. He never looked very comfortable out of doors but he said, 'Quieter out here.' Then he raised his glass and added, 'Cheers.'

'Cheers,' I echoed. So it wasn't sunshine and it wasn't under-age drinking. He had picked somewhere private to talk.

He put his glass down carefully on the slightly sloping table and fished his wallet out of the inside pocket of his jacket. There was a small, sharp bulge in it. 'I've been carting this about,' he said. 'Kept meaning to give it to you.' He took out a small object wrapped in a twist of paper and put it in my hand. 'It was your granny's,' he said. 'My mother's. I hope it will fit you.'

It was a thimble. When I unwrapped it I saw that it was solid silver, with an incised pattern like interlaced cobwebs.

'Oh, Dad!' I said. 'How did you know? Barbara Golding said I must look for a good thimble of my own.' I put it on the third finger of my right hand and it fitted perfectly.

He smiled. 'Silly how you keep these things,' he said.

Then there was a long silence. I examined the thimble with minute closeness and put it on and took it off several times, and smiled at Dad and looked away again. He drank some beer and put his glass down carefully. 'So you're getting on all right there, are you?' he said. 'Early days yet, of course.'

'Oh, it's fine,' I said heartily. And there was silence again. I drank a little of the shandy and remembered the disastrous party. This time last week it hadn't happened.

'I've known Joss since we were boys, you know,' my father said. 'We went to school together though he was a bit older than me. His father and mine being in the same trade, I suppose there was a bond between the families. Your mother never really liked it, you know. Can't blame her, I suppose. She was ambitious – wanted me to meet the right sort of people.'

I didn't want to talk about Mum. Not yet. So I just said,

'Yes, Joss said you were old friends.'

'He's a crafty old devil,' Dad said affectionately. 'Doesn't miss much. He said a funny thing to me on the phone the other day. When he rang up about you.'

'Oh, yes?' I said casually. 'What was that?' But a tightening in my stomach warned me that we were approaching the hidden subject. Dad had more courage than I did.

'He said he thought you were worried about something,' he said. 'Something to do with me.'

I had to tell him. Now.

'Well,' I said, and it sounded like someone else's voice, 'You told Mum there was a good restaurant in Soho, up the stairs by a betting shop.' He nodded, looking at me intently. 'I went there with Nick,' I said. 'On Friday last week.'

I didn't have to say any more. He put his hand over mine. 'What a thing to happen,' he said. 'I'm so sorry, my dear.'

Now that I had broached the subject, it was easier. 'It's all the Abrahams' fault,' I said. 'I didn't mean to tell them anything about it but somehow they got it out of me and they explained a bit about it. Laura Sheridan.' It sounded funny to say the name aloud after days and days of repeating it to myself.

He nodded slowly then gave a long sigh. 'So,' he said. 'What do we do now? You haven't told your mother – no, of course not.' He gave a faint, unhappy smile at the thought of the way things would be if I had told her.

'I nearly did,' I confessed. 'It was a kind of awful curiosity. I asked her how she would feel if you were having an affair.'

'What did she say?' he asked keenly.

'At first she said she'd feel totally let down,' I told him. 'As if she'd sold out everything else she might have been, for nothing. And then later she came and said if I ever thought you *were* having an affair, I must tell her. She said she'd rather know.'

'Sold out,' repeated my father. He leaned back in his chair and stared, frowning, at the glass of beer he held on the table. Then he said, 'You'll think this sounds horribly commercial, but after all, a deal is a deal. If you want one thing, you give

157

up another. When you were very small I had the chance to go into the silk trade. It would have meant being based in Hong Kong, travelling a lot in the Far East, buying for a consortium in London, Joss Abraham among them. It's the kind of thing I'd always hankered after. But your mother hated the idea.'

'So you didn't go,' I said.

He did not bother to reply. After a bit he said, 'I'm not excusing myself. I should have realised it was what people call an affair, with all the overtones of guilt. I've known Laura so long, you see. I don't know how much Joss and Myra told you.'

'Quite a lot,' I said. And then I heard myself blurting out, 'I know why you married Mum, for instance.'

He looked away quickly. I stared at the asters with their warm, sad colours, and wished I had not said it. I could have waited. After all, we would have plenty of time, Dad and me.

'They're lovely people, the Abrahams,' Dad said, 'but they do like to be involved in people's lives. No idea of conventional English reticence.' He sighed and looked at me in concern. 'I ought to have told you.'

I shrugged. I'd been thinking about it a lot. 'If I'd known,' I said, 'it would have been much worse. In some row with Mum – I'd have mentioned it. Or she would. And that would have been awful.'

'Perhaps,' said Dad. He looked helpless. A deal was a deal. He had kept his side of the bargain and controlled every other side of it, too, as well as he was able to. You couldn't ask for more than that.

There was silence for a little while and I knew he was thinking about Laura. Trying to work out what to do. I didn't want to say anything. He had apologised to me for touching on a painful subject when we were walking along the road to come here. I did not want to commit the same blunder.

He smiled at me, but it wasn't a real smile. The pain behind it made me want to cry. 'I'll explain to Laura what's happened,' he said. 'She'll be very upset that we've caused you this distress. We've talked about it so often – the risk of hurting other people. But it seemed all right.' He picked up his glass as if to drink out of it, then put it back on the table. 'She'll understand,' he said. 'We won't meet again.'

I looked at him but he would not meet my eye. He was sitting with an awful stillness and then I saw him shake it off. He picked up his glass and this time he drained it, replacing it on the table with the same terrible care.

'It feels like losing a leg,' I said. 'Or half your brain. A huge part of yourself.'

He looked at me and said, 'Oh, Sasha.' It was the first time he had used my chosen name. 'Do you know that already?' He shook his head. 'It's a painful thing to learn.'

'Is that the way you feel about Laura?' I asked him, and after a pause he said, 'Yes. But you don't have to worry about it any more. I'm terribly sorry it happened.' He looked at his watch and added, 'We'd better get back. I can see why your mother gets cross, stuck in the house, making gravy.'

'She doesn't *have* to cook in the middle of the day,' I pointed out, and picked up my thimble carefully from the table as I finished my drink. I was thinking hard.

I took my father's hand as we walked home, and remembered seaside holidays, bare-footed and trailing a spade that bounced and clattered over the sandy concrete as I trotted by his side, holding his hand.

I said, 'You must tell Mother.'

'No,' he said.

'Yes, you must.' I made him stop and look at me. 'Dad, I'm grown up now. If she thinks she can't live with you any more because of it, then we'll all have to face up to that. But she's got a right to know. She's not a possession. She's a real person. She's got to be able to choose and she can't do that if she doesn't know the truth. You must tell her.'

He closed his eyes for a moment, and I knew how he felt. We walked on.

'You know what it may mean, don't you?' he said.

I nodded.

'I love your mother very much,' he said. 'That's the awful thing. Life doesn't always settle neatly round one person as a focal point. But I can't have you in the middle, knowing

159

about it all and forced into taking sides, keeping secrets. No, I'll have to do as I said. It's the only way. Then you can forget all about it.'

I stopped him again. 'I *can't* forget about it,' I said. 'I'll always look at you and think of your unhappiness, and what's going to happen if Mum and I have a row? What if I let it out accidentally? I'm not a controlled person – I'm like Joss and Myra, I have to say what I feel. I'm not threatening you – God knows it's the last thing I'd want to do. But I don't know if I can keep it to myself for ever. I'm not strong enough. And it would be so awful if I blurted it out in a temper. You must tell her, Dad. You've got to.'

'Oh, God,' he said.

We came round the corner and for a moment I almost stopped. Nick's bike was standing outside the house. My own words rang in my mind. If he keeps coming round I'll keep seeing him. He had chosen for me.

Dad didn't notice the bike. 'I'll have to pick a time when we're alone,' he said as if to himself.

I said, 'I think perhaps you'll have this afternoon.' This time he glanced at me and saw me looking at the bike.

'Now, don't you go rushing into anything because of me,' he said anxiously. His grip on my hand tightened and he stopped once more and turned to me, frowning. 'Do be careful, my love. I don't want you to be hurt.'

'Don't be silly,' I said, and smiled at him rather sadly. 'We've got to live, haven't we?'

And then we walked on towards the house in the quiet autumn sunshine.